MELTDOWN

MELTDOWN

Ray Kytle

DAVID McKAY COMPANY, INC.
NEW YORK

MELTDOWN

Copyright © 1976 by Ray Kytle

Library of Congress Cataloging in Publication Data

Kytle, Ray.
    Meltdown.

    I. Title.
PZ4.K996Me   [PS3561.Y8]   813'.5'4   76-10209
ISBN 0-679-50576-8

MANUFACTURED IN THE UNITED STATES OF AMERICA

For
Kara and Katie

PROLOGUE

SOME EIGHTY FEET in depth, more than one hundred fifty feet wide at its rim, the enormous man-made crater resembled a stage prop for a lavishly budgeted science-fiction movie. Partially erected steel trusses towered out of its depths; thrusting skyward like the denuded stalks of gargantuan bouquets, clusters of slender rods swayed faintly. The bottom of the crater was littered with jagged concrete footings, indeterminate mounds of material, massive machinery—and men. Like an infestation of ants, the laborers swarmed among the detritus on the bottom of the pit, and above it as well, on an all-enveloping web of scaffolding. Only the sloping earthen ramp through the far side of the crater suggested potential escape, thereby mitigating the impression of some inhuman, extraterrestrial hell. Five months after the ground-breaking ceremony, such was the appearance of the Sand Beach nuclear-power plant.

At the bottommost concavity of the crater, amid the deafening cacophony of construction, Apprentice Plumber Clyde Jones took his anger out on a pipe fitting. One more year as an apprentice, he consoled himself—eleven months and two weeks, to be exact—and then he'd have his own helper to dump on. Till then, he had no choice but to shut up and take it. He gave the pipe wrench a vicious shove, and felt the threads go. Stripped. Just like that. And at quitting time, no less.

The whole section would have to come out. Not tomorrow, today. Tomorrow the pipe was to be cemented in. So there went his date with Darlene.

Still squatting, he removed the wrench from the pipe fitting. Dreyer, he knew, would be waiting for him to turn around, ready with that superior smirk of his. "You did it," he'd say, "now you fix it." And then Dreyer would sit on his butt for three hours collecting overtime while he, flunky Jones, pulled the whole section out and put in a new one.

He was goosed, hard. As he sprang to his feet, he heard

Dreyer laugh. "Wanna make like a monkey, go to a zoo," Dreyer said. Jones ignored the insult. The son of a bitch hadn't noticed.

"Quitting time," Dreyer said. "You finished?" When Jones gave a curt, surly nod, Dreyer went to fetch the Inspector.

Jones felt no anxiety. It wasn't the sort of thing the X-ray could detect; it was the sort of thing you were supposed to report.

The Inspector trundled over his machine, held the scanner over the joint, and studied the image briefly. "Okay," he said, making a notation on his clipboard checklist.

Jones turned his back on Dreyer, stepped out of goosing range, and began to pick up his tools. As he sorted them into the toolbox, he grinned to himself. If that piece of luck wasn't an omen, nothing was.

* * *

Ben Hogan knew he should have shut up when he realized Ross was determined to go ahead with the scheme, but couldn't help himself. It was a nuclear plant, for Christ's sake. "We could go to jail," he said.

"Nobody's going to jail," Ross said. "Get that idea out of your head." Rising from his chair, Ross placed his hands flat on the desk top and leaned across it toward Hogan. "I tell you, the Inspector's a fool: he goes by the book. The book says he's supposed to check every tenth load, so the jackass takes a sample from every tenth truck. I've watched each delivery. He samples the first truck, then the tenth, then the twentieth, and so on. He's a machine.

"I didn't know the Deerfield quarry would go bad on us," Ross continued, shifting abruptly from reassurance to rationalization. "The cores we took at the beginning were fine. I'm not the one who jacked up the price of lime fifty percent since we bid on this damned contract—we stand to lose a hundred grand. I'm not about to drop that kind of money just because of some quality-control horseshit."

Hogan turned his eyes away from Ross's choleric face to

4

gaze at the serpentine line of dusty mixer-trucks that crowded the cement plant's five-acre yard. In his mind's eye he could picture the drivers grousing: What is this, anyway? This business of getting in line, keeping your place, being checked through the gate in a certain order?

Some, he knew, would suspect. Not the whole operation—that required knowledge they didn't have. No, just that something was fishy. But none of them would really care. It was a job, it paid well, and others had to do the dirty work. Two years ago the union had forced through mandatory air conditioning for the cabs. So they could care less if Ross wanted to pay them to sit on their butts and smoke in cool comfort while he made like a cowboy rounding up a wagon train.

"What if the guy doesn't do it like before?" Hogan said, turning back to face Ross. "What if he decides to spot-check?"

"I'll be watching," Ross said. "If he takes a sample from one of the wrong mixers, I'll call you. Then you phone him with a bunch of bullshit about a foul-up. The son of a bitch will be grateful. He'll be able to blame you, you can blame the dispatcher, and I'll cover for the lot of you."

Ross moved around the corner of the desk and stepped forward to give his plant manager a fatherly slap on the shoulder. "Quit worrying, Ben," he said. "It's going to work."

As it turned out, Ross was right. The deception went off without a hitch. Over a ten-day period, the Hillsdale Cement Company provided fifteen hundred tons of coarse, highly porous, inadequately limed cement for the foundation of the Sand Beach fast-breeder reactor.

*   *   *

No one suspected that Phil Evans was a sick man. Even Phil Evans himself did not realize just how sick he was—nor was he about to do anything to find out. In only fifteen months more he would be eligible for the full two-thirds retirement benefit. He planned to wait two or three weeks after that time, and then go to the Company doctor. If he did it now, he knew, they would get him out on one-half plus disability. In the long haul, two-thirds plus disability would make one hell of a difference. He could fake it till then.

Kneeling before the bank of circuits in the Diesel Generator Room of the Sand Beach power plant, he closed his eyes for a moment, praying that when he reopened them all would be in focus and the squirmy wires would lie still and have quit changing colors.

This was his third reactor, which was why they had picked him in the first place. He was experienced, which made him fast, and speed was what the contractors wanted. And then there was the premium pay that went with the job, money he could well use with his retirement coming up. To the Company, the assignment was a favor, a plum; there was no way he could have refused without raising suspicion.

Slowly, cautiously, he opened his eyes. His vision was better. Not good, but better.

He clipped the voltmeter to the next pair of poles and systematically continued his circuit check. So goddamned many, he complained to himself as the wires, smokelike, again began to writhe. No wonder he had a headache. But everything seemed to be coming out right. Thank God for that.

Even as he offered up that grateful thanksgiving, Evans understood that, had things not come out right, he could never have retraced and corrected his error. He just wasn't capable of doing it—whatever it was that plagued him was getting worse.

House wiring was no problem for him. He could wire a house in his sleep; or an office building, for that matter. But no more reactors. He made a penciled note of the voltmeter's reading beneath the appropriate terminal on the wiring diagram. Yes, it was all checking out.

What Master Electrician Phil Evans did not realize was that he had cross-wired two critical sensors for a seventy-five-foot run of the primary and secondary power conduits. Since system functioning was checked by throwing master control switches at the various electrical panels, the mistake went undetected. All the circuits still functioned; they all tested out.

The potential for disaster created by his error was really quite small. But it did exist. Should power to the core-coolant pumps be interrupted in the miswired segment, the interruption would not register on Control Room instrumentation, nor would the reactor scram—that all-important emergency shutdown mechanism—automatically be triggered.

For more than three years, these facts mattered not at all.

REACTOR YEAR ONE
SAND BEACH

1

DR. PAUL HANSON—Phi Beta Kappa, Yale; Ph. D. in Nuclear Physics, M.I.T.; post-doctorate Atomic Energy Commission fellow in fast-reactor safety—first viewed the Sand Beach nuclear plant from the air. Peering through the plexiglass bubble of the Consolidated Power helicopter, he caught sight of the installation while they were still twenty miles away. At that distance, only its sparkle was visible, a diamond in a setting of jade. But as the helicopter drew closer, the plant grew more defined, and more beautiful: a symmetrical mating of form and function.

The two enormous cooling towers were the first features to take on a separate existence. Red-and-white-striped, like candy canes, to enhance their subsidiary function as navigational aids, the twin towers rose almost two hundred feet toward the sky. Some hundred feet in diameter at the base, the towers tapered gracefully to a diameter of forty feet, then, for the upper one-third of their height, flared gently outward again to form mouths sixty feet across.

Almost simultaneously, Paul was able to distinguish the radiant white crown of the reactor's containment dome. That first view of a nuclear reactor's dome was a sight that never failed to move him. For the containment dome, unlike the other structures of nuclear-powered generating plants, was immutable. Though such reinforced concrete domes varied in size depending on the power of the reactor over which they arched, that was their only variation, and even that was slight. Always glistening white, always vast, these symmetrical hemispheres were, for Hanson, emblematic. Both sign and symbol, they bespoke the elemental power of nuclear fission, and man's triumphant achievement in mastering that power. The fact that this technological triumph, unlike so many others, had not spawned ugliness, but led to the creation of

11

beauty such as he was now viewing, seemed to sanctify his chosen profession.

Their landing approach was over water, and as the distance lessened, Paul understood the appropriateness of the plant's designation—for sand beach there was, glistening white and extending north and south for miles along the lakeshore. And, behind, green pine forest. He found the plant a stirring sight, its immense power tamed and harnessed, embosomed silent and radiant amid natural splendor.

"There's the pad," the pilot said.

Hanson peered down toward the spot indicated. All the details were now clearly visible. Between the trees he could see the black ribbon of the access road. It debouched into a car-speckled parking lot, beyond which lay a wide swath of landscaped lawn. From north to south, parallel to the shoreline, were the cooling towers, the domed Reactor Containment Building, and the Administration Building. Around this elemental triad clustered the smaller but essential outbuildings: the Reactor Service Building, the Plant Service Building, and, farthest south, the Generator Building. Still farther south, umbilically attached to the Generator Building, stood the gigantic transformers, double fenced for security. From that fenced enclosure, an arrow-straight line of steel-girdered, cable-draped power towers marched inland to the southeast, toward the metropolis Sand Beach had been built to serve. Almost unconsciously, the clue the stately march of the waves beneath, Hanson deduced that this was also the direction of the prevailing winds.

They were descending stage center, near the south side of the main Administration Building. On the helipad below, Hanson made out a foreshortened figure clutching its head.

This was a beautiful area, he reflected. Sherry would love it.

Plant Manager Ron Claton stood on the tarmac of the helipad, well away from the outermost ring of yellow concentric circles which marked the proper touchdown point, observing the approaching helicopter's transmutations as it grew from gnat to fly to crow to buzzard to bubble-beaked pterodactyl. This fellow Hanson he was about to meet was the third candidate for Operations Supervisor they had sent him, and he was determined to make a good impression.

He hadn't been told why the first two men had declined the job, nor had he asked. There was no reason to assume it had anything to do with him. Still, enough was enough—a few more refusals and people would start talking. Travis, Regional Manager, Southeastern District, would be the one to start it.

"Heard about the trouble up at Sand Beach?"

"No," the other would say. "Can't say I have. But aren't they behind on their start-up of the reactor? Seems like I read something in the Company newsletter about full operation by June, in time for the summer."

Then Travis again. "They can't get an Operations Supervisor. You know Ron Claton? He's the Plant Manager. Seems that all the physicists they've brought in can't stand him."

"I'll be damned."

And then it would begin to spread—idle gossip at first, soon simple fact . . .

"Heard about the trouble up at Sand Beach?"

"Yeah. Somebody mentioned it to me. Claton can't get a physicist."

"Nice promotion coming up for somebody."

"Yeah." Laughter. Then, tentatively: "I never liked him much, myself."

"Pushy S.O.B., if you ask me."

"Yeah." Shared laughter. End of Stage One.

Then, Stage Two: "Hi, Cal. What brings you up here?"

"Nothing special. Just wanted to get away for a couple of days. Told Hammond I'd heard good things about that new scrubber in your cooling towers and wanted to check it out. Say, what's this about Claton being fired?"

"Supposed to happen any day now, from what I hear. They couldn't find a single physicist in the whole damn country who would work for the bastard."

In Stage Three, the self-fulfilling prophecy would take over, transforming rumor into reality.

"Why isn't Sand Beach into its start-up?" one of the senior Vice-Presidents would ask.

"We're still looking for an Operations Supervisor. We've sent five candidates out there to look it over, but each one turned us down."

"Any reasons? That's a pretty place. Should get one out of five, at least."

"No reasons. Just 'Thanks, but no thanks.' "

"Well, that's kind of fishy, isn't it, no reasons? Who's in charge out there?"

"Ron Claton. Seems like a good man. Made Plant Manager in six years."

"That's moving right along, isn't it? What's the average?"

"I'd say ten years, ten or eleven."

"Maybe he's pushy. Coming on too strong and turning off the applicants."

"I don't know."

"Check into it. Ask around. We can't have that plant just sitting there."

"Right."

"Do we have someone to replace him?"

A moment's thought. And then, mention of a protégé. "Keith Harris over at Big Rock."

"Okay. Look into it and let me know."

"Will do."

No way, Claton resolved as the prop wash from the descending chopper beat against the muted blue of his tailored suit. The lines of his jacket were accented by a single red thread that etched the borders of lapel, pockets, and cuffs, adding, Claton thought, exactly the right degree of color, a befitting touch of flair. His close-cropped black hair, impregnated that morning with a double dose of Stay-Fast in anticipation of this very windy arrival, was scarcely ruffled. Nevertheless, as he worked at his welcome smile, he raised his right hand to help hold it in place. He was a man who valued a neat appearance.

The appearance of the burly man clambering out of the

helicopter was scarcely neat, but it did hold a certain unpretentious appeal. As Hanson lumbered across the tarmac, bending over lest his head be lopped off by the helicopter's idling blades, their clatter now reduced to an intermittent whoosh, Claton was reminded of a shaggy bear—the kind of trained circus bruin that drank soda pop from a bottle: friendly, and eager to please. For Hanson was wearing a broad, half-chagrined smile, obviously conscious of the awkward figure he cut. Not knowing whether or not he was clear of the blades, Hanson kept his head-down hunch until he was only a few feet from Claton. When he suddenly straightened up, Claton took an involuntary step backward, as if a grizzly had abruptly reared before him. At least six foot two, the Plant Manager calculated, about two hundred thirty pounds, and with an unruly mane of salt-and-pepper hair that any bear would be proud of.

"I'm Hanson," the man said, extending Claton a friendly paw.

Claton clasped the hand, found it held no claws, and resuscitated his smile of welcome. "Ron Claton," he replied. "Plant Manager."

Introductions completed, there was a moment of discomfort as the two men smiled at each other, each waiting for the other to make the first move. As host, Claton decided, that move was properly his. He motioned in the general direction of the Administration Building, to help Hanson get pointed in the right direction.

"Let me show you around," he said.

An hour later, they left the executive wing, where Claton had just shown Hanson the spacious suite that went with the position of Operations Supervisor. As they approached the pair of plate-glass doors which separated the executive offices from the Control Room proper, Claton surreptitiously glanced at his reflection and straightened his tie. So far, so good, he thought. Hanson seemed favorably impressed by what he had seen. In planning the tour's itinerary, Claton had deliberately put inspection of the Control Room last—the icing on the cake, so to speak. As the place where Hanson would work, his area of special responsibility, Claton hoped it would be the clincher.

To enhance this effect, Claton had lagged behind at the doors, letting Hanson take it all in undistracted by his presence. That accomplished, he strode to the center of the room.

"All the very latest," Claton observed. "The very best." Actually, he only partially understood the operation of half the instruments in the room. The remainder he didn't fathom at all—but he wasn't expected to. Reactor Control was Hanson's thing; his was overall plant management. He reminded himself that one could scarcely manage a plant that wasn't operating. If he could snare Hanson for the job, reactor start-up could begin within a week.

Hanson nodded absently in response to Claton's observation. It was true—in terms of instrumentation, the plant was a showpiece.

He stepped up to the main control panel and rested his right hand on the back of the black leather Danish armchair that would be his if he accepted Consolidated Power's offer. Picturing himself sitting in that comfortable, commanding chair, monitoring and directing the operations of the plant, harnessing its enormous power, he experienced a pull far stronger than he had anticipated. Faintly embarrassed, not entirely sure of the force compelling him, he swiveled the chair toward him, sat down, and on its solid, silent bearings swung around to face the control panel.

Though he recognized the notion was absurd, he nonetheless felt a surge of proprietary, almost jealous, possessiveness. This was the command post being offered him, and he liked the way it felt. He would take the job.

16

2

PAUL HANSON had a pretty fair notion that he hadn't been Consolidated Power's number one choice for the position of Operations Supervisor at Sand Beach. All the signs pointed to his being third or fourth down the list: the start-up-ready condition of the plant, Claton's undisguised eagerness that he accept the position, even the munificence of the salary. But in no way did that suspicion dampen his ebullience. He had been blessed by a fluke of fate. In his daily calls back home, fearful of tempting his beneficent deity into withdrawing its favors, he told Sherry only that things looked favorable. When he saw the verbal agreement in hard, black print—when he held the contract in his hand, signed, sealed, and delivered—then he would allow himself to believe, and tell Sherry that the job was really his. He spent the four days until the signing house hunting. On the afternoon of the fifth day, he met Sherry at the airport and drove her straight to his discovery.

"Well," Paul said. "What do you think?" He had planned this moment as a tribute to his wife, bespeaking his deepest, most heartfelt gratitude. He wanted it to say "Thank you"— thank you for bearing with me these last six years; for putting up with sterile, noisy, cramped university housing without complaint; for doing menial slave-work to supplement my crummy stipends; for enduring the loneliness of my daytime class-work and nighttime laboratories; for denying yourself the child you've wanted so badly all these years. He wanted the moment to express all these things. When Sherry turned to him, he realized just how successful he had been. Radiant with joy and love, she was sobbing.

Murmuring his name, she began to cry in earnest, succumbing to her happiness. He held out his arms, and she clutched him, shuddering against his chest.

The real-estate broker, cut off in mid-sentence by Sherry's

sudden tears, stood in the center of the room gaping at her. Then, mumbling an awkward apology, he found a door and vanished.

Paul felt Sherry brushing her face against his suit coat, and realized she was drying her eyes. A moment later, she lifted her face and gave him a full, searching kiss. "You bear," she said. "You sweet, sweet, wonderful bear." Taking his hand, she led him to the sliding doors at the rear of the living room, a forty-foot expanse of plate glass opening onto a cedar-planked balcony. Standing together on the balcony, they gazed down on a lush terrace, a pearl-drop swimming pool beyond, and a perfectly manicured lawn sloping gently down toward a frothy, pine-shaded stream some three hundred feet away. Arms entwined like new lovers, they let the glorious panorama wash over them.

Even though this was the fifth or sixth time he had stood there, the effect, Paul acknowledged, had not diminished—it was a truly magnificent house in an incredibly beautiful setting. The similarity to Sand Beach suddenly struck him. Like the nuclear plant, this sparkling villa also resembled a diamond amidst jade. In a way, that was fitting, for the one had brought the other. Like twin halves of the same august event, they were inextricably related.

"Of course," Sherry said, "We can't really afford it." She smiled at him, assuring him that she didn't mind.

"Wrong," Paul corrected. "We can. The appraiser put the value at a hundred ten thousand dollars. But it's in an estate with something like two dozen heirs, and they're all fighting. Twenty thousand here or there is just a few hundred more or less for each of them—and they want a quick sale. We can get it for eighty thousand."

"But we don't have a dime," Sherry protested.

"Guess what they're offering me for moving expenses?" Paul grinned. " 'Relocation Bonus,' they call it."

Sherry regarded him with bemused skepticism. "What?"

"Guess," Paul demanded.

"How do I know?" Sherry exclaimed. "Besides, we don't have anything to move."

18

"Guess," Paul repeated happily.

Smiling, Sherry determined to go outrageously high. "Three thousand," she said.

"Higher," Paul said.

"Five thousand," Sherry ventured dubiously.

Paul shook his head. "Higher."

"But we can move our stuff for less than five hundred," Sherry protested.

"Higher."

"Eight thousand."

"Higher."

"Ten thousand."

"Higher."

Sherry released his hand and turned to stare at him. She looked incredulous. "Higher?"

"Higher," he said.

"I can't," she murmured. "I just can't."

"Fifteen thousand!" Paul exclaimed. "And forty-seven as a starting salary."

Sherry began laughing and crying simultaneously. "Do you know how much we made last year," she choked, "what with my wages and your fellowship both?"

"About nine thousand," Paul said.

"And you're telling me we're going to make almost sixty-five thousand dollars this year?"

"That's right."

"And I can get pregnant?" She was like a child on Santa's lap. Suddenly, everything was possible.

"Tonight." Paul laughed.

In the motel room the next morning, Paul woke to find Sherry sitting propped up by pillows against the bed's headboard, with a thermometer in her mouth, a pencil stub in her hand, and a pad of paper on her lap. Face aglow, she smiled enigmatically around the glass tube. The filmy, semi-transparent blue negligee rucked up about her thighs served more to accent than to conceal her sex.

As Paul watched her, he felt the quality of his erection

change, reflexive morning tumescence hardening with object and intent into purposeful desire. Like a witching wand quivering toward water, dragging the diviner along behind it, his stiffening prick pulled toward its own favored well, turning him until he lay on his side facing her.

The thermometer still between her teeth, Sherry saw his condition. Arching an eyebrow, she cupped his member in her hand and stroked its head in compassionate sympathy. The result was not solace but agony.

"Help!" Paul gasped, grinning.

"Mmm," Sherry mumbled, suddenly releasing him to reach for the thermometer.

Like a swollen baton, dropped, his penis plopped against her thigh, gave a yearning spastic throb at the soft contact, and then, as Sherry continued to study the mercury, recognized that it had been spurned. In little slithering jerks, it began a retreat.

That withdrawal, whether strategic or merely tactical, nevertheless allowed Paul's mind to paw past the heat of groin and begin to function for the first time that morning. The problem was that Sherry had become more and more beautiful through the years of their marriage, until now, at twenty-six, her tiny body—one hundred five pounds of scented softness standing scarcely five feet three—resembled a perfectly proportioned Barbie doll come wantonly to life. Indeed, he often thought of her as such a doll, a woman with the slightness of a child. Where she found sufficient space to sheath his engorged shaft with such delectable facility remained to him a marvelous mystery.

Its head still purple with frustration, the diminished creature between his legs stirred hopefully, encouraged by the direction his thoughts had taken. But, having lost round one, it was unable to regain the initiative.

"You're not really sick, by any chance?" Paul asked. He watched as Sherry finished making a notation on the pad propped against her thighs and then placed thermometer, pencil, and paper on the night stand beside their bed.

20

"Mmm," she murmured, shaking her head. She was smiling mischievously.

"But you're taking your temperature."

"Mmm." This time she nodded, just as vigorously.

"Why?"

"I have to." She was grinning now. "Every morning."

Her delight at his puzzlement was contagious. Paul sat up, crossed his legs, faced her, and joined in the game of "Guess What I'm Up to Now."

"Why?" He grinned.

"Because I'm making a basal-body-temperature chart."

"And just what does a basal-body-temperature chart do?"

"It tells me when I've ovulated. Just after I ovulate, my normal waking temperature will shoot up almost a full degree."

"And then?"

"And then," Sherry exclaimed, "you've got to screw me!"

Paul kept his grin, but felt a bit nonplussed, nonetheless. To make love on impulse was their way, and he had assumed that such spontaneous desire would also suffice to make Sherry pregnant. He found this dry science a bit unnerving. His limp member, moments before so eager, confirmed his assessment. "I don't blame you," he commiserated in silent sympathy.

He pictured the inevitable future scene: Sherry, jostling him awake, clutching the thermometer, nodding judiciously. "It's gone up!" she would proclaim. In his mind's eye, he saw a three-color diagram of female anatomy, like a sketch from some manual for would-be plumbers. "Now get it up and stick it in and fertilize the thing," she would command. "Quick! Before it dies from malnutrition." And there he would be, half awake, groggy with fatigue, sex the last thing on his mind, and the least desired, expected to rise to the occasion.

"Ugh," he said. He was still working to keep his smile, but it was fading despite his efforts. "It sounds so mechanical."

Sherry lunged at him, knocking him flat atop the bedsheets. Before he could recover, she had straddled his chest, pinning his arms behind his head. Her pelvis was just inches from his face, at eye level. "But you'll do it," she growled with mock ferocity.

Effortlessly breaking her grip on his arms, he pulled her down on top of him. But even as she dropped to his chest, she slithered backward, brought her head above his groin, and caught the head of his penis, at half-mast and rising, between her teeth.

"Ahh!" he yelled. The cry was involuntary, evoked by his member's terror. His partial erection withered.

"Say you'll do it," Sherry growled, without loosening her jaws. She had also moved one hand to his balls, gripping them with equal threat.

"I'll do it! I'll do it!" Paul cried, capitulating. Smiling up at him with bright triumphant eyes, Sherry maintained the dual pressure for an instant longer, just for emphasis. Then he felt the teeth move away, replaced by gentle lips and a caressing tongue.

"You're a bitch," he said, laughing as his muscles relaxed. He began to move his hips, meeting Sherry's engulfing mouth motions, and let his head fall back.

"You're not going to get it night and morning like this from now on," Sherry gurgled a while later. "We've got to wait thirty-six hours between times—to keep your sperm count up."

Paul opened his eyes and met her smile. "Fine," he said. "Whatever you say." Then he pushed her head back down. "Just don't talk with your mouth full."

START UP

3

THE INITIAL start-up of the Sand Beach reactor required nearly seven months. Many would have found the cautious procedure dull, the rigid routine, followed scrupulously week after week, maddeningly monotonous. But to Paul Hanson, it was fascinating.

In the course of his fellowship, he had spent two full months behind a control-room simulator, so, in a sense, it was all old hat for him. But despite the realism of the simulator, this was different—this was real.

The reactor operators whom he supervised seemed similarly awed. It was as though they were timorous Lilliputians fearfully arousing a slumbering giant. The giant must not be abruptly or rudely wakened, lest, in a single thrashing spasm, he destroy them all. Instead, he had to be eased into wakefulness, gently and slowly, in such a manner that his docility would be assured.

Like the myriad ropes which rendered Gulliver helpless, they too had a means of constraint: scores of control rods with which to harness the latent power in the Sand Beach reactor core. To suddenly withdraw those rods, like abruptly severing Gulliver's bindings, would allow the giant to lash out, precipitating disaster. Hence the lengthy, meticulous procedure by which the reactor was brought up to full power.

The control rods would be retracted gradually, millimeter by millimeter, until finally, deep in the reactor vessel's subterranean core, criticality was achieved. Then, ever so cautiously, the rods would be withdrawn farther, allowing the core to become momentarily super-critical. The power output, a direct function of the thermal energy being generated, would rise quickly and the movement of the control rods would be reversed once again until a stable, self-sustaining nuclear reaction was achieved, now at a slightly higher power level than before. They would repeat this laborious and delicate process,

25

interspersing each step up the power scale with myriad tests, checks, and recordings, until eventually the reactor's power output reached an operational level.

Precisely because this start-up procedure demanded that the reactivity in the reactor core repeatedly be raised to supercritical levels, it was regarded as the most dangerous aspect— "sensitive phase" was the euphemism—of nuclear-plant operation. It was not enough that the personnel conducting the operation were highly trained specialists who could be trusted to proceed with caution. Safety dictated that there be a backup system, a fail-safe technology, that, while capable of being triggered by human hands, was simultaneously superior to and independent of the fallible judgment of mere mortals. Thus, in addition to the control rods—reactivity-damping devices capable of controlling the reactor in the course of normal operation—the Sand Beach reactor was safeguarded by twelve massive, magnetically controlled scram rods.

Stainless-steel-clad cylinders three inches in diameter and twenty feet in length, the scram rods were held above the reactor core by powerful electromagnets. Gleaming in the Reactor Room's harsh, perpetual light, these rods resembled gigantic stillettos poised above the reactor's heart, ready to subdue the slightest show of rebellion by stabbing downward. And, indeed, to kill instantly was their sole purpose.

There were as many ways these daggerlike safety rods could be unloosed as there were conceivable threats to the reactor. In this respect, the scram rods were murderous saviors. For, in some untoward event, only killing the reactor, instantly snuffing out the reactivity which was its life, could prevent it from destroying itself in an uncontrolled nuclear power excursion.

To guard against such a catastrophe, there were all varieties of automatic emergency shutdown systems: a temperature scram, a reactor-period scram, a power-level scram, an air-exhaust-stack scram, a radiation-detector scram, a core-coolant-pressure scram, a core-coolant-level scram, a loss-of-electrical-power scram, an earthquake scram, even an intruder

26

scram, which would automatically release the scram rods if doors to key areas of the plant should be forced.

It was difficult, perhaps even perverse, to entertain the notion that such a magnificent constellation of safeguards might somehow fail, and during these start-up months, and for many months thereafter, such a notion never crossed the mind of Operations Supervisor Paul Hanson. He did notice, and filed a *pro forma* report on the matter, that the Sand Beach reactor was characterized by an exceptionally brief period, or "e-folding time"—the number of seconds in which the reactor's power output would increase by a factor of e, the base of Naperian logarithms. He also found the delayed Doppler effect that resulted from the new fuel-pin design a bit unnerving. A reduced Doppler coefficient, in conjunction with such a brief reactor period, seemed to be shaving the safety margin a bit thin. Nevertheless, in both cases he rationalized away his misgivings. His job was far too fresh and far too exciting to allow time for doubts.

Above all, there was his impending fatherhood. Sherry's mathematical approach to fertilization had justified her faith, and she was now orchestrating her pregnancy with the same earnestness that had marked her approach to insemination.

Again, just as with the home they had purchased, Paul was conscious of an almost metaphysical mating of his professional and private worlds, as though Sand Beach were a doppelgänger of his and Sherry's own nuclear family. It required no particular poetic sensibility to perceive the analogy between the life in the bowels of the reactor he was working to quicken and the life quickening in Sherry's womb. In fact, the two processes had become so inextricably intertwined for him that he half expected Sherry's parturition to exactly coincide with the reactor's attainment of full operational power.

These thoughts refocused his attention on Sherry, and he realized he had lost the count.

Lying on the living-room carpet, her back propped up by sofa cushions, Sherry was practicing the breathing technique for the first stage of labor by the Lamaze method. Paul, kneeling beside her, was supposed to be timing the simulated contractions.

"Contraction ends," he announced arbitrarily, releasing the pressure of his hand against her thigh. She glanced at him with faint puzzlement, then returned her eyes to the focal point while taking the mandatory cleansing breath.

"Are you sure?" she asked after the prolonged exhalation. "It seemed shorter than the others."

Smiling down at her, Paul confessed, "Actually, I lost count. Let's do it again."

While she rearranged the cushions behind her back, he marveled at the taut balloon of her stomach. She had told him that the last two months would bring the greatest growth. That the tiny waist he remembered could accommodate still further stretching seemed incredible. Already her bellybutton had disappeared, replaced by a slight surface irregularity, like a vaccination mark on the arm or thigh. When he had commented on the change, she had laughed: "First time in my life I've been able to get it really clean."

Jesus, he thought to himself, if he had something so big in his stomach, and growing all the time, he'd be scared stiff. For eventually it had to come out. And through a channel so narrow that even his prick could enter only with a shove.

"Hey," Sherry said. She raised her left arm and waved a hand back and forth before his eyes, like a hypnotist trying to determine whether her subject was in a trance. "You all there?"

Paul gave her a smile of chagrined apology. "Sorry," he said. "Are you ready?"

When she nodded assent, he gripped her leg just above the knee, glanced at the second hand of his watch, and began to squeeze. "Contraction begins," he announced.

Sherry took a cleansing breath, began *effleurage*, and started to pant in fast, shallow breaths. As Paul bore down on her leg with steadily increasing pressure, simulating the increasing intensity of a contraction, she breathed more and more rapidly.

28

"Fifteen seconds," he said, exerting more pressure. "Thirty seconds."

Sherry's breath came in shallow, quickening gasps. Her unfocused eyes looked through him as she concentrated on keeping the *effleurage* synchronized with the quickening tempo of her breathing.

"Forty-five seconds," Paul announced. He glanced at his hand, and saw that his knuckles were white with the pressure he was applying. She should be crying out in pain, yet she seemed oblivious to the pressure.

Feeling a bit guilty, and not a little amazed, he rapidly eased the pressure as the second hand completed its sixty-second sweep. "Contraction ends."

Without interrupting her self-administered abdominal massage, Sherry took another deep cleansing breath, exhaled, and then let her arms fall to her side. "How did I do?" she asked after a moment of relaxation.

"Fantastic," Paul said. Bending over, he kissed her lightly on the lips. "You're going to be the star of the delivery room."

4

HANSON REALIZED that he had forgotten to breathe, and exhaled noisily. Glancing at Pete Owen, the Senior Reactor Operator, seated before the control panel to his left, he saw a blanched face, and wondered if his own features were similarly drained of blood.

"Christ," Owen said, more to himself than to Hanson.

Hanson kept a wary eye on the Period Meter even as he grunted in sympathetic agreement. If the power surge had lasted just five milliseconds longer, the reactor surely would have gone prompt critical.

"Don't thank Jesus, thank Doppler," he said. The joke was a poor one, but he didn't know how else to react. In this sterilized, pressurized, fluorescent-lit room, a paean to man's mastery of nature, one could scarcely get down on bended knees and give prayerful thanksgivings. Yet that was precisely the action their salvation seemed to warrant.

Hanson was not a religious man, or a superstitious one. If compelled to choose, he would probably have styled himself an agnostic, though he was more indifferent to religion than skeptical. Nevertheless, there was something about this huge reactor that was beginning to make him uneasy, as though man were transgressing beyond his limits, flaunting his vanity. For a brief moment, Paul entertained the absurd notion that the barely controlled power transient they had just experienced was a cautionary admonition from on high.

"Well." Owen grinned. "It's like they teach you in school. If you're going to ruin one of these things, chances are you'll do it in start-up." Paul noticed that Owen, despite his apparent flippancy, was still monitoring the Neutron Counter, the one instrument that would signal a new power surge as quickly and accurately as the Period Meter.

The near excursion had just begun to register with the other personnel in the Control Room, a dozen Junior Reactor Operators and various assistants. Their confusion resulted from the fact that their manipulation of certain control rods had suddenly been usurped by the two men at the main control panel, by means of an emergency override never before employed. They knew that something had gone very wrong, but not what, or how, or why, or to what effect. The normal silence of the Control Room was broken by the buzz of their speculation.

"If she'd coughed up a few more neutrons," Owen added, the forced quality of his banter becoming increasingly obvious, "we'd know by now whether or not the scram works."

Paul nodded in grim-faced agreement, and saw Owen abandon his grin. The near-runaway was no laughing matter. He'd have to write up a report on it, too.

That unhappy thought—the prospect of hours of paperwork as a consequence of a two-second incident—brought him back to the business at hand. That business was to bring the reactor up to operational power. He instructed Owen to disengage the override that had castrated the junior operators. The momentary power burst had been terminated successfully, no harm done. It was time to return to routine.

5

GARBED IN A BLUE surgical gown, wearing sterile cloth slippers over his shoes, his hair tucked into a special cap, and with a gauze mask covering nose and mouth, Paul held Sherry's hand as she was wheeled toward the delivery room. He tried to smile reassuringly with his eyes.

They had not been spared the usual horror stories: true case histories of friends and acquaintances who had been betrayed. There were tales of doctors who at the last moment reneged on their solemn pledges and excluded the husband from the delivery room; tales of unsympathetic, tradition-shackled nurses who forced gas on the protesting mother-to-be while the physician pretended preoccupation; tales of needless spinal injections administered without warning, robbing the laboring woman of the sensations required to monitor her own contractions; tales of women whose arms and legs were needlessly bound by leather thongs, whose chests were strapped flat to the delivery table, making both controlled breathing and pushing nearly impossible.

And, of course, in office visits and at physician-attended group lectures, they had endured the counterpoint: scarcely credible fables about husbands which, like apocrypha, allowed the offending physicians to rationalize. If he had not heard of them with his own ears, the stories repeated with somber pomposity by half a dozen staff physicians and nurses, Paul would scarcely have credited their existence. Like stock characters in some outrageous melodrama, they appeared with grotesque predictability in virtually every meeting with hospital personnel.

Paul had devised labels for these aberrant fathers so often cited by the doctors to rationalize their routine. There was, most incredibly of all, yet most often alluded to, Pervert. Pervert was not really interested, so the story went, in helping his wife. His dark motive was to peep in at other women in labor and on the delivery table. More than once, it was claimed, a nurse had returned from her station to find Pervert prowling the halls and seeking jollies, having forsaken his wife to indulge his unnatural lust.

If Pervert was the type most repugnant to the nurses, Fighter was the physicians' bête noire. Fighter did not skulk, he attacked. He would assault the doctor in the delivery room itself, always at some critical juncture of a suddenly crisis-ridden childbirth. It was probably mordant jealousy, the doctors speculated sagely—Fighter could not bear the sight of another man's hands on the intimate parts of his wife's anatomy.

Scarcely less unsettling to the staff was Fainter. Like Fighter, and Pervert too, for that matter, Fainter could seldom be detected in advance. Well hidden, he quavered in even the most masculine men, revealing himself only in the delivery room when, as was always the case in these accounts, the life of both mother and child hung by a fraying thread.

And so it went, more stereotypes of psychotic husbands out of control, and a whole repetoire of hysterical women, too. The message, Paul reflected, came through loud and clear: "Doctor knows best." A sly mixture of condescending paternalism and blatant self-serving egotism, that dictum was, to Paul, totally lacking in credibility.

About half the couples in the early meetings where this message was purveyed had succumbed—one saw them no more at the Lamaze classes. For them it was to be the tradition-hallowed knock-'em-out-and-drag-it-out routine. The other half, to which he and Sherry belonged, stuck it out, searched for the right doctor, tried to get as firm a promise as possible, and prayed it wouldn't all go to shambles when those promises were put to the test.

Sherry smiled and squeezed his hand in return, letting him know his message had been received. Then, as another contraction began, she took a cleansing breath and started the pant-blow exercise.

Paul felt strange—at once preternaturally close to Sherry, yet simultaneously detached, like a disinterested observer. Without really anticipating trouble, he was nonetheless determined that nothing, absolutely nothing, should go wrong.

He was not overimpressed by the much-vaunted goal of sharing the childbirth experience, so extolled in their Lamaze class. This was, inevitably, Sherry's moment, not his. His role, as he conceived it, was to do everything in his power to insure that the experience for which Sherry had so carefully prepared herself would not be denied her.

And it would have been denied her, he reflected later, had he not been there. All would have been taken from her, senselessly, by that ancient, stone-faced leviathan of a nurse whom they had come to loathe during Sherry's protracted labor. For no sooner had the battle-ax and her sycophantic assistant transferred Sherry from cart to delivery table than the woman grasped Sherry's left wrist and moved to strap it flat against the table's side. The aide followed her lead on the right.

Their action, coming without warning or words, interrupted the practiced *effleurage* with which Sherry was pacing the pant-blow sequence. Startled, she lost her rhythm and involuntarily tensed, and what had been a managed contraction was instantly transformed into a wrenching, painful spasm.

The doctor, his head lowered between Sherry's draped thighs, saw nothing until Paul's protest drew his attention. He glanced up briefly. "She doesn't have to wear those," he told the assistant nurse, and went back to his examination.

Paul was trying to unshackle Sherry's left wrist when he felt her twist in the midst of another contraction. Looking up, he found the ancient nurse doggedly striving to force a cupped gas mask over his wife's nose and mouth. Sherry was trying to elude the mask by shaking her head from side to side.

"No gas," he said, pushing the nurse's hand away.

The obstetrician looked up at Paul's exclamation, took in the situation, and directed the nurse, "Let her hold it. She can give herself gas if she wants it."

The nurse slapped the mask into Sherry's hand without

looking down, her eyes fixed on Paul. He glared back at her with equally grim dislike. She was vanquished, and knew it. Paul suspected that she hated the doctor, too. For he was to blame for her defeat, allying himself, as he had, with these outsiders. It was bitter bile to swallow.

Whenever he thought back on the delivery, it was always this confrontation that stood out most vividly in his memory— more vividly, even, than the other disjointed, phantasmagorial flashes into which the half-hour or so had been compressed: Katie crowning; then her head dangling free between Sherry's thighs, her skull all purple beneath matted brown hair; then, all in a rush, the rest of her suddenly, magically, free of the womb, two persons where an instant before there had been but one; and finally Sherry's beatific smile as the infant, no parts missing or misplaced, was set at her breast.

REACTOR YEAR THREE

CRY WOLF

6

THIRTY FEET below ground level, in the sub-basement of the Diesel Generator Building, Lester Cuthright sat on a brick-work shelf, chewing at a dry, tasteless sandwich. His straw-blond hair, greased, cut a knife-edged ledge above his forehead; pencil-thin sideburns, close-cropped, accented the narrowness of his sallow face. To a casual observer—or, for that matter, even to an interested one—Cuthright's attitude seemed both natural and typical. His lunch pail open beside him, he was slouched back against some ductwork. His right arm appeared relaxed, dangling at ease behind the knee-high shelf on which he sat. Some one hundred yards away, in the Administration Building, a Security Control officer was seated before a three-tiered bank of closed-circuit television monitors. The only thing the officer saw was "poor ole Lester" eating his lunch in his favorite spot.

The penknife which Lester was using to dig out the mortar around the second brick down from the top of the shelf was invisible, as were the small, quick wrist motions by which the job was being accomplished. The red bandanna handkerchief into which Cuthright had ostentatiously sneezed, apparently stuffing it back into his hip pocket, lay beneath his hand on the floor, functioning as an improvised dropcloth. As Cuthright worked at the mortared joint, the handkerchief's pattern was gradually obscured by a gentle dusting of white powder.

In one respect, however, appearance and reality were one. For Cuthright seemed moodily withdrawn, preoccupied, almost dreaming—and he was. He was back in Tennessee, back in the hero days . . .

It had been like magic, those months. The Green Valley power plant going up, the full-page "Help Wanted" ads in the newspapers: any kind of help, every kind. And so it went, even as unskilled mason's helper making more cash than he had ever seen in all his twenty-four years. And then the future Senior

39

Reactor Operator, himself a good old boy made good—hanging around, trying to memorize everything—taking a liking to him, giving him a tip. "They've got to give first priority to local applicants. It's policy."

"Priority" not even in his vocabulary then, but the impossible dream opening up. Not to end when the bricklaying was over—just beginning.

"You apply. I'll write a recommendation. They'll train you themselves."

And him stumbling along behind, disbelieving, the title itself—Rad Protection Technician—like something out of a fairy tale.

"What does it mean?"

"You'll monitor radiation."

"How?"

"Easy."

"What?"

"No problem. Just apply. I'll take care of it."

So he did. And then they trained him, just as the man had said they would. There was nothing to it—snoop-probe-read-record—kneel-swipe-read-record. Take a reading, make a record; make a swipe, enter a reading. Any fool could do it. But most didn't know that.

"Hey, Lester. What ya doin'? Hear you're some big cheese out at the Plant."

And he, hero days: "Rad Protection Technician."

"No shit?" Laughter. But no sneer underneath. Impressed. Lester Cuthright, Rad Protection Technician at THE PLANT.

Rachel just sort of melted. His rivals gave up. She was his for the taking. They got married.

And then the incident. He could still remember the feel of it going in—prickly in his balls.

When he had tried to describe it at the trial, they had used it against him. Further evidence of his ignorance, they claimed. Irradiation wasn't something a person felt.

"Physiologic symptomatology evidencing preconscious awareness"—those were the very words one of the Company-called physicians had used. He remembered them because he had scrawled them down and later asked his lawyer what they meant. He still had the scrap of paper somewhere . . .

If only he had been able to show them, actually bring Eric into the courtroom and let the jury see what that dose of radiation had done to his son. But the judge had forbidden it, had even forbidden him to mention his boy at all. Eric's abnormalities were not at issue, he ruled. The concern, he instructed the jury, was whether the radiation dosage Cuthright had received was presumptively or evidentially genetically harmful. The burden of proof rested on the plaintiff.

Both the proof and the burden existed, did indeed rest on him—lay on him, in fact, with heavy soul-crushing oppressiveness. Yet that burden and that proof could not be displayed. Not, at least, before the jury's eyes. Only before his, at home— mewing, flapping the uncoordinated flippers that passed for arms, sightless, spastic. Two years old then, at the time of the trial; now, at five, exactly the same, only bigger—his son.

His attorney had advised an out-of-court settlement. Privately, he had told Lester, the Company admitted negligence. It was possible that Lester would contract leukemia or cancer. Statistically speaking, his life expectancy had probably been shortened by a few weeks, perhaps even by several months. They didn't really believe that—so they said—but they were willing to acknowledge that it was possible. They wanted him to be happy, and they didn't want the incident publicized. They were prepared to offer thirty thousand.

Lester knew it was hush money. But that wasn't why he refused it. He wasn't interested in scruples: he wanted revenge.

"Two million," he told his attorney. "That's what we're suing for." Actually, he would have accepted $1,000,000, maybe even $500,000. It had to hurt—that was the whole point. One million hurt, though not enough. No amount would really hurt enough. But $30,000 was nothing to them—not a scratch, not an itch, nothing.

In stages, through a protracted series of "final" offers, the Company worked its way up to $100,000. At that point, when Lester still remained adamant, it balked.

"You're not even alleging a clearly demonstrable tort," his attorney had complained. "It's all hypothetical. There are too many variables, too many other possible causes for Eric's condition. If the jury awards just on life expectancy, you'll be lucky to get half of what they're offering. And that's assuming we can prove negligence. If the case comes to trial, they'll deny culpability."

"They've gotta pay more than that for what they did to Eric," Lester had replied.

When, on the very eve of the trial, the company had suddenly upped its offer to $150,000, he had rejected the proffered settlement with the same words.

In *Cuthright vs. Consolidated Power Company*, the jury had found in favor of the plaintiff and awarded him $40,000 in "full and final settlement" of all claims arising from the incident at the Green Valley nuclear plant. The amount of the award reflected the jury's rejection of that portion of the plaintiff's claim alleging permanent and severe chromosomal damage. The parade of healthy males put on the witness stand by the defense, all of whom had received radiation dosages as great as or greater than Cuthright's, and all of whom had subsequently sired one or more normal, healthy children, convinced the jury. The testimony of these men, however, had had no effect whatsoever on Lester. In his view, they had simply lucked out.

By the time the trial ended, Lester's attorney had gained some slight, imperfect insight into the workings of his mind, a vague inkling that Cuthright did not reason in the same way as most of his clients. Perhaps it was that vague, uneasy intuition that led him, in their final post-trial consultation, to try to convince Cuthright that he had really cost the company a million dollars after all.

But Cuthright would have none of the lawyer's complicated extrapolations of total man-hours involved, cumulative salaries paid, witnesses compensated, and dollar-valued goodwill lost through adverse publicity.

"They ain't paid," Cuthright had told him.

Occasionally, as he munched his lunch and picked away with his penknife, Lester Cuthright smiled. In Security Control, the officer scanning the closed-circuit television monitors noticed one of these smiles and became fully alert. The log showed several personnel working on the ground floor of the Diesel Generator Building, but Lester was the only employee recorded as having entered the lower levels. Whoever he was smiling at was in violation of procedures and regulations.

Pushing buttons, the officer swung the remote-control television camera toward the spot Lester had smiled at. Nothing. He followed up with a quick yet complete scan of the room. Still nothing.

Yet when the monitor returned to Lester's face, he was still smiling, and at the same empty spot. With a sigh of sudden comprehension, the security officer restored the camera to automatic scan and, like Lester, smiled with self-satisfaction. Poor ole Lester, he thought, dreaming away. He could not imagine, though, anything in Lester's life to smile at.

Until last Tuesday, eight days ago now, Lester would have agreed with the security officer's assessment. In the three years that had elapsed since the trial, his life had grown bleaker than before. The older Eric grew, the more difficult and wearisome caring for him became. And with Rachel now drinking almost continuously, each daily homecoming held the promise of some new, unthinkable disaster. A few random scenes presented themselves and, in the instant their suppression required, turned his sandwich fetid. No, there was nothing to smile about there.

It was his week-old discovery that was pleasing him, or, rather, the anticipation of making a long-hoped-for discovery. For the Company had still not paid. And as the price he paid for its criminal negligence had increased, the payment he meant to extract in return had similarly grown.

He now realized that the mere money restitution he had demanded earlier was insufficient, and was glad that demand had not been met—a mutually agreed-upon settlement would have bound him. The so-called settlement the court had made had settled nothing. Coming from outside, forced on him, it left him free.

The redress he now sought must cripple the Company as surely and inevitably as the Company had crippled him. And just maybe, at three forty-five last Tuesday afternoon, he had found the way . . .

Snoop-probe-read-record. Snoop-probe-read-record. He could do it in his sleep—had been, in fact, doing it half asleep last Tuesday. For there was never anything to record, never any change—just the same background radiation day after week after year.

As he had come to understand the basic workings of nuclear-power generation—not through any deliberate effort at self-improvement or ambition, but simply through ongoing association with those who did understand and talked about it—he had eventually come to share the scorn for his job almost universal among the professional reactor staff. For his job was futile, useless, absurd. The Sand Beach installation contained thousands of individual radiation monitors: radiation disks worn by every employee; radiation counters in every nook, cranny, and corner; radiation sensors on virtually every pipe, fitting, loop, link, and rod in the Plant. Radiation monitors everywhere—automatic, computerized, transistorized, foolproof. And yet here was he, fumbling Lester, Radiation Protection Technician, poking around with a hand-held survey meter like an old stumblebum uranium prospector out of the 1950s.

When the stranger entered the Diesel Generator Room, Lester's cursory glance at his identification tag was triggered by mere conditioned reflex. The need to scrutinize any unfamiliar person for proper identification had been drilled into all plant employees. The name on the tag read "C. Hinkley."

"Howdy," the man said. "The *C*'s for 'Chuck.' "

Lester nodded without interest, and started to turn back to his work. But the man was holding out a paw. Reluctantly,

Lester raised his own arm and made the handshake. "Lester," he said.

"Cold as a witch's tit in here," Chuck exclaimed with a broad smile.

Lester recognized the breed. "You from Montana?"

"Wyoming," Chuck said.

Close enough, Lester thought. Montana, New Mexico, Wyoming—they all said "Howdy," liked to grin, and talked too much. He nodded and turned away.

"Don't mind me none," Chuck said. He banged his toolbox on the concrete floor and rummaged noisily. "Gotta test some circuits."

Lester made another swipe, then recorded time, place, and identifying symbol on his clipboard.

"Seems the regular guy's on sick leave," Chuck said. "I've been doing these tests six days now. Never seen so many panels in my life."

When Lester declined to fill the pause following this bit of information, Chuck began to whistle. Lester recognized the melody of "Laredo."

"Started with the hot-leg pumps in the Reactor Building and been working my way back ever since," Chuck observed when he finished the tune. "After this, I go over to the off-site transformers, and then I'm done."

Down on his hands and knees, groping to make a floor swipe in a machinery-obstructed corner of the room, Lester missed a few sentences of the man's prattle. But his tone of voice came through. He was speaking faster, and in a higher pitch. Lester smiled faintly. Talkers got on his nerves, but he got on their nerves, too, so it all evened out. The swipe completed, he backed out, rose to his feet, and tuned in again.

"Yes, sir," Chuck was saying. "If a fellow wanted to screw things up, this is where he would do it."

For a moment, Lester went rigid. Then, deliberately, he made his shoulders slump, his arms and hands go loose. Half turning around, he played pen over clipboard as though writing.

"How's that," Lester drawled. His eyes, veiled with

45

studied disinterest, rested on one of the auxiliary diesels to his right. Tone and expression said he could care less.

Chuck stooped down, fitting the voltmeter back into his tool chest. When he straightened up, he swept his hand toward the constellation of steel conduits against the room's whitewashed cinderblock wall. Four one-inch-diameter pipes entered the electrical panel from above, two more from the side. Beneath, two larger pipes about two inches in diameter, ran down toward the floor, then curved through a sleeve in the wall. Two other two-inch-diameter conduits, unconnected to the switch box, disappeared through the same hole.

"Wouldn't have seen it myself," Chuck said, " 'cept for the way I traced it all back."

Glancing at the man's face for an instant, Lester made a shrug of bored incomprehension. It was encouragement enough.

"They've got it all separated," Chuck said. "Real clever." He gave Lester another one of his cowpoke grins. " 'Cept for right here." He pointed at the hole. "Right here it all runs together, off-site and on-site power both."

"So what?" Lester repeated. It came out a challenge, almost hostile. Actually, he knew "so what." Or thought he did. He suspected the man was telling him that he could get around all the carefully engineered backup systems and take out the reactor's primary-core-coolant pumps with a simple little explosion. But it seemed incredible.

Chuck laughed. "So what?" He squatted and pointed at the sleeve he had indicated earlier. Stepping closer, Lester went down on his haunches and followed the man's pointing finger. The sleeve was actually the end of a five-inch steel pipe; all the smaller pipes ran into it.

"There they are," Chuck said. "All four powerlines for the pumps."

Glancing at his wristwatch, Lester saw that it was almost one P.M.—time to clean up his mess. He clicked his penknife shut, palmed it, and, pretending to rummage, dropped it into his lunch pail. The handkerchief was more difficult, and took more time—he mustn't spill the mortar. But once the corners were folded over, it was just a matter of slipping it into his hip pocket. He figured six or seven more lunch hours before the brick would come free.

7

ACTUALLY, FIVE WEEKS passed before Lester finally felt the brick wobble. He had been saved by janitor Joe Grimes, a buddy, insofar as Lester could or would style any person a buddy. He and Joe took turns picking each other up for work, and on Friday afternoons they would stop off for a couple of beers before going home. Occasionally, if one or the other suggested it, they would stop for a drink after work in midweek. That Wednesday afternoon, mellow with the progress he was making, Lester offered to buy.

They never talked much anyway, so ordinarily Joe's fidgety silence wouldn't have bothered him. But since he felt good, he wanted to make conversation, and Joe's reluctant mumbles weren't doing the trick. He had to prod, finally getting downright angry, before Joe could be persuaded to say what he had wanted to say all along.

"How a man spends his lunch break ain't nobody's business but his own, far as I can see," Joe muttered grudgingly.

Lester felt scram alarms ringing all through his body. He nodded slowly, looking down at his beer. When Joe didn't continue, he drawled, "So?"

"No skin off my back, you wanta be alone, eat by yourself," Joe observed.

Lester looked hard at his friend and nodded. Both men pulled at their beers for a while. Then Lester said, "Somebody makin' it his business?"

Joe shrugged. "Probably don't mean a thing."

"Probably not," Lester allowed. He surveyed the bar idly, as though bored, then signaled the waitress.

When the barmaid had come and gone, Joe began peeling the bottle's label with his thumbnail. That gave his eyes something to watch while he said what he had to say. "Yesterday noon I was pokin' around in Security, cleaning things up. You was already eatin', and Dirk, he was watchin' you on the monitor." He flicked his eyes to his friend's face for an instant before returning them to the beer bottle's shredded label.

" 'You say he's been eating there every day for a week?' I heard him ask the fellow on duty that. 'Every day since last Wednesday,' the fellow said. Then Dirk, he made a sort of grunt, and put his hands on the back of the man's chair, and leaned over him, and just sort of watched you on that screen. Still at it when I left the room."

"Dirk's been tryin' to nail me ever since I come here," Lester said.

Joe nodded understandingly, without looking up. "Just thought maybe you'd wanta know," he said.

It wasn't until after he had dropped Joe off and headed toward his own house that Lester sensed how late he was going to be.

Even on Fridays, it was two quick beers and home before six. Because six o'clock, at the latest, was when Rachel expected him. She tried—he had to give her credit for that. And, usually, she was able to make it.

"Don't be late," she beseeched him almost every morning. Blowzy in a faded bathrobe, puffy-faced, clutching a mug of coffee he suspected she dumped down the drain the moment he left, she daily made her fearful plea, a plea that held a special meaning, both a promise and a threat. For she did make an effort to hang on till he returned; that was the promise. The threat was more hopeless than hostile, simply the other side of the promise. He glanced again at his watch. Even with the help of the dinner-hour-thinned traffic, it was going to be after seven when he got home.

He prayed she'd be all right. Tonight, of all nights, he needed to think, needed peace and quiet—to plan.

Even as he took out his latchkey, he could hear Eric's convulsive screams, the sound penetrating right through the closed door. With the door opened, the terror-filled wailing clamored against his ears.

He took two steps into the small vestibule, then turned

49

right into the dusky, curtain-shrouded living room. No Rachel.

Momentarily, he felt a surge of hatred. If she was in the kitchen, swilling, just letting Eric scream . . .

But she wasn't. He found her on the far side of the sofa, on her back. The bathrobe had come open, exposing half her torso, mottled thigh merging with swollen stomach in rolls of jaundiced fat. One pendulous breast lay flaccid across her ribs like a varicose-veined sow's teat, dropping almost to the floor. An enormous blood-crusted bruise swelled across the left side of her face.

He stared down at her for several seconds before she registered his presence. "Fell," she slurred. An arm rose weakly toward the television console, and slumped back. "Couldn't get up." Her words were barely audible above the din of Eric's screaming.

Lester nodded. Even standing above her as he was, the stench of liquor, mixed with acrid sweat, was overpowering. "You're okay," he said, not bothering to add, "just blind drunk." She knew that already. He gazed down at her expressionlessly for a moment longer, then turned away.

When he reached the top of the stairs, Lester hesitated, steeling himself. Then, with three brisk strides, he reached the door to Eric's room, and entered.

Without glancing toward his son's barred bed, he moved directly to the wall cabinet and took out a disposable plastic hypodermic syringe. Stripping off the sterile wrapping, he plunged the needle into a rubber-capped jar of sedative. Only then, properly armed, did he turn toward the thrashing, screaming creature in the cagelike crib.

"It's all right," he murmured tonelessly. "It's going to be all right."

Nevertheless, it was only by sitting on his son's back that he was able to hold him sufficiently still to swab an area of buttock clean of feces and then jab in the needle.

Eric quieted almost instantly as the drug took effect. When the boy's convulsions had subsided to choking, reflexive sobs, Lester picked him up and, indifferent to the vomit and excrement smearing his shirt front and pants, carried him to the bathroom. He ran a few inches of tepid water into the tub and carefully bathed his son. That done, he returned him to the bedroom, laid him on the carpet, and put fresh linen on the bed. When Eric was finally tucked in, Lester changed out of his soiled clothers. Altogether, it took about forty-five minutes.

Back downstairs, he found Rachel just as he had left her, only now she was snoring, slack-jawed. Lester got a blanket and covered her. Then he went to the kitchen.

Since there was no debris, he deduced that Rachel had neglected to feed Eric any supper. But there was no changing that now. Without the drug, Eric would have been too hysterical to eat; with it, he could not be kept awake. Maybe around two o'clock, Lester thought; by then the drug would be wearing off. He'd set the alarm.

At nine forty-five he finished washing his dinner dishes and was able to sit down and think about what Joe had told him.

8

PAUL WASN'T SURPRISED that Sherry's first words after her welcome-home kiss were "What's wrong?" In the early years of their marriage, he had been able to mask his moods, but after almost nine years of intimacy, she saw through even his most determined efforts.

Yet, in all those years since they had first met, he had never lied to her. It was not a record he dwelled on pridefully, nor did it issue from any righteous self-conception of being one of the world's moral stalwarts. He simply had never encountered an occasion that demanded deceit. Not until now.

That this first abuse of Sherry's trust should arise from embarrassment was in itself embarrassing. Yet it was precisely such chagrin, the fear of appearing a fool, that led him to insure privacy and prevent her questioning by lying.

"Nothing is wrong," he replied. "It's just that I had to bring home a batch of paperwork. A bunch of crap." He attempted a martyred smile. "Where's Katie?"

"In her bedroom. Taking a nap."

Paul missed her, missed the delighted "Daddy! Daddy!" with which, these last months, she had greeted his daily homecoming.

"Mix me a drink while I take a peek at her," he said. "A Manhattan." When Sherry's look remained skeptical, he added, "Really. It's nothing. Just paperwork."

Upstairs, gazing down on his sleeping daughter, Paul acknowledged that he had become a hopeless sentimentalist, a living, breathing stereotype. The mist in the eyes, the lump in the throat, the knot in the pit of the stomach—all the clichéd symptoms of the doting father were his.

Katie lay on her back on the quilted cover of her bed, a bottle tucked under one arm, her favorite doll under the other. Her wispy blond hair, already shoulder-length, seemed to float about her head. He noticed she was wearing the duck outfit, her favorite: red pants and a matching blouse, with a yellow cloth duckling stitched across the front.

What struck him most was her fragility, her almost absolute vulnerability—and the fact that she seemed totally unaware of that defenselessness. *He* realized how vulnerable she was, how many ways she could be injured or killed, how completely her life depended on the careful control of circumstance—but she herself did not partake of that terrifying knowledge. Indeed, if the psychologists were to be given credence, she saw herself not as powerless, but as omnipotent; not as vulnerable, but as invulnerable. A trauma would be any event that abruptly shattered that illusion. Yet illusion it was, and shattered, in some fashion, inevitably it must be.

Perhaps this was the key to the core of his difficulties at the Plant. For as this small, fragile life had been placed in his custody, and as he had come to recognize how utterly dependent upon him and Sherry that life was, a parallel awareness had grown, a realization that millions in the environs of the Sand Beach Nuclear Plant dwelled in a similar childlike state of blind and ignorant bliss. Innocent of dread, of any sense of threat, of any knowledge of their own helpless vulnerability, they, like his daughter, went about the serious business of existence completely ignorant of how easily, effortlessly, and arbitrarily they could die.

He turned away from his daughter and descended the stairs. In the living room he found Sherry waiting. Whether because the curtains had been drawn against the glare of the afternoon sun or because of his mood, the once marvelous room had lost its magic, indeed, seemed mundane. Grimacing to himself, he accepted the drink Sherry offered him and moved to an armchair. Settled comfortably, he took his first sip from the glass, sighed, and prised off his shoes.

Sherry had not moved. Standing in the center of the room, where she had met him with the drink, she was watching him intently.

An old dog uncomfortable with a new trick, he abandoned the effort at deception. "There's no paperwork," he admitted. "I said that so I could go up and read some stuff without telling you what or why." He gazed at his wife, tense now, not knowing what to expect, clearly confused, but, even more than that, scared, unable to comprehend what he could possibly be leading up to. "I think the goddamned Plant might blow up," he said.

An hour later, Paul entered his upstairs study, quietly closed the door behind him, and walked reluctantly to his desk. For a few moments, instead of sitting, he rested his hands against the back of the chair and gazed out the window above his desk at the snow-shrouded lawn and distant winter-denuded trees. He had never found beauty or pleasure in snow, regarded all winter sports with distaste. The nature he loved was green, not white.

Turning aside, he stepped over to the bookshelf against the wall to his left and scanned the titles. The work he sought was on the next-to-top shelf, sandwiched in among half-forgotten textbooks dating back to his undergraduate days. There were dust smudges on his hand when he pulled it out.

Seated at the desk, he positioned the book before him: Dr. Howard C. Thompson's *Explosion Potential of the Liquid-Metal-Cooled Fast-Breeder Reactor*. Nuclear-power interests regarded the book's author with all the affection General Motors lavished on Ralph Nader after the publication of *Unsafe at Any Speed*. Burden, bane, and scourge, Thompson had provided a cathartic focus for their collective outrage. To suffer fools was their inescapable fate; but to put up with Thompson and his insufferable hypothesis was demanding too much. Let God forgive him; they, human, would hate.

For Thompson had a thesis. Put quite simply, it was that the liquid-metal-cooled fast-breeder reactor, or LMFBR, as it was usually abbreviated, was potentially a mini-atomic bomb.

Formulating that thesis to himself, Paul Hanson did not smile, as his employers would have both wanted and expected. He knew Thompson's monograph well: he had read it in its original form as a doctoral disseration, as well as in its published form. And, like most physicists with a vested interest in the commercial development of the LMFBR, he too had found

Thompson's argument flawed. For it demanded that one accept as credible certain reactor-fuel behaviors—"configurations" was the technical term—which were statistically improbable. But Thompson himself acknowledged that fact. His contention was that, however improbable, such configurations were theoretically possible. And that contention Hanson could not, then or now, refute. Nor, he reminded himself, had anyone else been able to refute it.

The Nuclear Regulatory Commission, the private utility companies, the plant managers, operators, and physicists—in short, Hanson reflected, everyone who knew enough to know—all recognized that the entire issue of reactor safety ultimately led to the question of explosion hazard. In this respect, those placard-bearing protestors who brandished their scrawled, totally predictable slogans at the construction site of every new nuclear plant were, despite their ignorance, correct—at least in their essential fear. If a nuclear reactor was a potential atomic bomb, then "Keep the bomb out of Bakersville"—that recurrent admonition which varied only with the city's name—made sense. At least, Paul amended to himself, some sense.

Yet there was a curious, even pathetic, irony in the popular fear of a nuclear reactor's supposed explosive potential. And, Hanson bitterly noted to himself, there was a definite element of self-serving hypocrisy in the response nuclear-power interests made to this widespread concern. For in even the largest nuclear reactors—plutonium-fueled fast-breeders like Sand Beach—the maximum blast potential was, by modern military standards, minuscule. Even Thompson's estimate of twenty thousand pounds of TNT equivalent was small compared to the size of tactical nuclear warheads, and no worse than the explosive potential of half a hundred chemical plants scattered across the nation. Fact, simple fact—and one the industry promoted with unflagging zeal: "A nuclear reactor is not a potential nuclear bomb." And so the populace was soothed.

"Well, if you're really certain it can't explode, it must be safe." That tended to be the reaction of those who accepted the official line. Those who didn't persisted in believing that such a claim was simply a self-serving lie; while the gullible might swallow it, they weren't so easily bamboozled. Both groups, Hanson reflected, were equally misguided.

The real danger was not blast but breach. A breeder reactor like Sand Beach, after some three years of virtually continuous operation, contained in its core a concentration of radioactive fission products equivalent to the fallout that would be released by the dropping of several hundred Hiroshima-yield atomic bombs. An explosion of only two thousand pounds TNT equivalent would be sufficient to breach the reactor vessel, blasting its head and the refueling machinery bolted to it right through the containment dome. Such an explosion would inevitably inject a large proportion of the vaporized radioactive core into the containment dome, from which it would leak into the atmosphere. The populace in the vicinity of such a breached dome would not die a fast, painless death by explosive blast; it was unlikely that anyone would die as a result of the actual explosion. Retching, diarrheic, blistered, they would succumb in slow agony as a result of acute radiation poisoning.

All of this was common knowledge to those involved with the nuclear-power industry, and to thousands of informed scientists and citizens not directly involved. Still, it aroused little concern. Except for a handful of fanatics, it was generally regarded as irrefutable that an explosion of two thousand pounds TNT equivalent within a reactor core was simply not credible. And since only the incredible could perpetrate the unthinkable, there was no point in dwelling on either.

His own personal dilemma arose, Hanson wryly acknowledged, from the simple fact that he had abandoned the ranks of the self-styled realists and wandered, without any conscious intent, into the ranks of those whom the realists called nuts.

With an abrupt change in intent, Hanson shoved Thompson's monograph, unopened, to one side of his desk. There seemed little point in rereading arguments he knew virtually by heart. The crucial question concerned not hypothetical effect but probable cause. Without a precipitating cause, there could be no cataclysmic effect. He selected another text from the bookshelf beside his desk and found the Atomic Energy Commission's staff-review statement. It characterized the AEC's position regarding LMFBR safety: "The safety program has as its objective the understanding of phenomena related to hypothetical events and their consequences which will provide *realistic* bounds and estimates of risk."

Dwelling on that official qualification, which he had mentally italicized as he read it, Hanson came to see it as a calculated out, a bit of cunning foreshadowing, like a clue in a mystery novel by which a later event was to be explained and justified.

"Just look," they could say. "Right here on page thirty-four of our report dated June nineteenth. We didn't make any guarantees."

Remembering, he rummaged through some old folders in the desk file drawer until he found what he was looking for: minutes of the International Conference on Sodium Technology and Large Fast Reactor Design held in the early seventies at the Argonne National Laboratory. The file was labeled ANL-7520. On page three hundred fifty-six appeared the statement he had imperfectly recalled: "It is, in our view, unlikely that one will be able to design for the worst accident permitted by the laws of nature and end up with an economically interesting system, even after extensive additional research has been carried out."

He took the two key terms from the two reports—one government, one private—and played with them. Put together, with a dollop of cynicism added, the definition of "realistic safety measures" became those safety measures that cost no more than the utility companies were willing to pay.

That's not cynicism, Hanson told himself, that's paranoia. But one inescapable fact remained: Sand Beach displayed a dangerously short reactor period, totally incongruent with its design. And nobody seemed to know why, or, for that matter, to care.

9

SAND BEACH Chief Security Officer Kenneth Dirk took his position and duties with deadly earnestness. Like Paul Hanson, Dirk was plagued by a nightmarish vision in which Sand Beach was transformed into a bomb—but one of much more familiar form than that which Hanson envisioned.

Dirk's waking nightmares had nothing to do with the sort of silent slaughter a radiation dispersal would cause. In his dreams, the Plant was not villain but victim. Skulking through those dreams were crafty anarchists, tract-brandishing true believers, grim-faced extortionists, duplicitous traitors, fresh-faced murderers, lean and hungry seekers of power—a troupe of kooks in every guise closing in malevolently on Sand Beach. And he, Kenneth Dirk, must spot them, foil their every machination.

In the three years that Sand Beach had been in operation, no evidence of sabotage or fuel theft, planned or attempted, had been unearthed. Nor, for that matter, had Dirk uncovered any such evidence at Big Rock, where he had worked as first assistant to the head of the security detail for five years before coming to Sand Beach. Of all the forty breeder reactors in operation across the country, there hadn't yet been a single incident of sabotage or subversion.

These statistics, so proudly trumpeted by the power companies as irrefutable proof of their airtight security, brought no comfort whatsoever to Chief Security Officer Ken Dirk. In fact, they had precisely the opposite effect. In Dirk's mind, the industry was a dumb poker player high on a winning streak, hot and cocky, betting on the come.

Dirk had done the same himself innumerable times—when you're hot, you're hot. No good poker player could afford to ignore a streak. If you didn't ride it, push it, milk it, it would desert you in disgust, offering its favors to a more lusty lover. But no matter how hard you rode it, you could be damned sure that it would finally go bust. So even though you had to use it, you could never trust it. In the end, it was all percentages.

And exactly because he was ultimately a percentage player, some eight months ago, for the first time in his life, the Chief of Security at the Sand Beach Nuclear Plant had asked a physician to prescribe some mild tranquilizers. The doctor was a young internist who had established his practice the same year Dirk had accepted the Sand Beach position. It would have been an overstatement to call them personal friends, but as partners on the same mixed-doubles bowling team, the men had developed a certain friendly relation beyond the merely professional. The doctor knew Dirk was happy in his marriage, comfortable with his kids, and no neurotic. He had written out the prescription without comment or question.

At League the following Wednesday night, it came out that the young physician had dropped negotiations for a wooded one-acre building site near the perimeter of the Sand Beach property. He had decided, his wife told Dirk's wife, that the neighborhood wasn't suitable.

Even as he rang the outer office and instructed his secretary to bring him Lester Cuthright's file, Dirk chided himself. James Earl Ray, Lee Harvey Oswald, Sirhan Sirhan—not one of them had had a rational, reasonable motive; not one had had a real grudge; not one had ever been identified in advance as a potential assassin. The F.B.I. had failed to prevent these murders because it had concentrated on obvious kooks, psychos who threatened but didn't act. The actors seldom threatened; they simply acted.

Yet here he was, falling into the same trap, repeating the errors he recognized so well. But not quite, he told himself. Cuthright had motive, even though he had never threatened. That cautious self-control made him suspect—even more dangerous. Cuthright was a failure. The title "Rad Protection Technician" was farcical, a high-sounding euphemism for a lowly, poorly paid, universally despised jerk—like the grandiloquent title "Sanitation Engineer" for a retarded garbage grub. All the men in the list he had just composed had been failures.

And Cuthright must have sex problems—why else would he have had a vasectomy? Never trust a man with sex problems—that was one of Dirk's precepts. Yet he was no puritan: he'd trust a happy homo over a hung-up hetero any day. But a guilt-ridden closet queen, an impotent lecher, or a self-castrated psycho: watch out. They often required a few corpses to get their rocks off.

Then there was the fact that Cuthright had nothing to live for—unless one considered hell living. A bloated drunk for a wife, a flipper-flapping freak for a son. Home sweet home.

Mainly, though, Cuthright had motive. A quiet, miserable, nothing-to-live-for, keeps-to-himself, sexually deviant man-with-motive was, in Dirk's estimation, a time bomb primed, charged, and ticking. Yet, despite it all, he could not touch the man.

His secretary's presence forced itself upon him. Taking the folder she held out to him, Dirk nodded dismissal without looking up. One more time, he told himself. Just one more time. There must be, there simply had to be, a way to nail the man—something that would justify his termination, even in the eyes of the union.

The union, Dirk repeated to himself with silent disdain. That was the problem in a nutshell. Without the protection of the union, Cuthright would have ceased to be a problem years ago.

"You don't like it? Lump it." That's how it would have gone, except for the goddamned union.

What kind of world was it, where a man could sue his employer, reject the most generous of settlements, drag his own company into court, create all sorts of damaging publicity—and still expect, and have the legal right, to remain an employee of the very same company he had dumped on? Yet, like it or not, such was the world they lived in.

"Termination for cause," that was the crucial clause. Somewhere, somehow, even if it required fifty rereadings of Cuthright's miserable file, Dirk was determined to discover cause. The percentages were getting to him. Sooner or later, they would prevail.

10

WITH INFINITELY painstaking caution, Lester worked the brick free. Since Joe's warning, he had dared eat his lunch in the sub-basement of the Diesel Generating Building only on that one day out of seven when the Plant's divisional directors held their weekly luncheon conference. As a result, the work of five days had stretched to five weeks—six weeks, actually. For he had not attempted to remove the brick when, toward the end of his lunch break exactly one week before, he had felt it move. Haste could ruin everything. Moreover, he wanted to savor the anticipation, the sense of imminent triumph that had made the last weeks fly by. And, should it turn out that he was wrong—that was a disappointment he would just as soon delay.

The room in which Lester sat was tiny by the gargantuan standards of the Sand Beach installation. No more than thirty feet by twenty, it was antiseptically stark: an air-conditioned, whitewashed shoebox of cinderblock and concrete. In the design blueprints it was marked "Reserved for Future Use," one of the two euphemisms popular with draftsmen to disguise waste space, the preferred designation being "Storage."

Three feet to his right, a gray fire door splotched the wall which separated the rectangular corridor from the Diesel Generating Room; it was behind that wall that Chuck Hinkley had shown him the electrical conduit. Some twenty-five feet to the left of where Lester sat, at the far end of the shoebox, there was an elevator, its enameled doors lemon yellow. Bolted to the wall next to the elevator, an emergency stairway of open steel grating rose through the ceiling. It resembled a fire escape, and although it led not down but up, that was precisely what it was.

Only two other features relieved the room's barrenness. One was the relentlessly swinging television camera mounted on the opposite wall, just below the ceiling, at the exact middle of the room. The shelf on which Lester had spread his lunch was the other. Two and one-half feet high, about the same in width, the shelf was constructed of russet firebrick and ran arrow-straight two feet out from the wall along the entire length of the room. Almost decorative in appearance, the shelving seemed mildly incongruous; in contrast to every other feature of the room, it had no apparent function. It looked like the afterthought it was.

The shelf did not exist in the original blueprints. The five-inch steel conduit housing the off-site and on-site power cables for the core-coolant pumps, and the electrically independent backup system for each, ran the length of the room in plain view, held rigid six inches above the floor by regularly spaced steel plates; ease of access and openness to visual inspection were by-words in nuclear-power-plant design.

At the mandatory Senate Sub-committee hearings where the Sand Beach design was reviewed, a notoriously anti-nuclear-power Congressman from an ecology-oriented North-western state had protested. The conduit was too vital to be left so open and unprotected. After all, who could tell what use the room might be put to in the future, or what heavy machinery might be moved through or into it?

A Consolidated Power architectural engineer had played with his slide rule and passed a note to the Company spokesman: the quarter-inch-thick stainless-steel conduit and interior piping could withstand a spot impact in excess of fifteen tons dropped from ceiling height. However, instead of communicating that information to the sub-committee, the Company spokesman had chosen to praise the hated Senator for his insight and agree that the conduit should be protectively enclosed. Placating the bastard with a brick shelf would cost pennies, and might shut him up. The shelf had been added to the Plant's specifications.

When he had worked the brick out about two inches, Lester paused to take a fresh grip. Then, in one smooth motion, he pulled it free.

For a moment, he simply held it. Despite all his planning,

success surprised him. Then, by pretending to peer into his lunch pail, he made natural the motion needed to lower the brick to the floor. The moment of truth had arrived. Whether or not he might have a reasonable shot at destroying Sand Beach, and thereby be avenged at last, could be resolved instantly by a quick poke. But Lester refused to be rushed.

Like all those ever employed at a commercial nuclear plant, Lester found totally absurd that dark figure so vivid to the popular imagination: the skulking, bomb-wielding saboteur who, through devious machinations, breaches security, creeps into the plant, blows up the reactor, and thereby unleashes a nuclear holocaust. A half-ton pickup truck loaded with TNT, parked next to the reactor's containment dome and exploded there, would have no effect whatsoever. The same quantity of explosives, carried case by hundred-pound case into the reactor room itself and then detonated—a process requiring hours of labor, during which, presumably, the entire plant staff passively observed—would also fail to achieve its end.

For the reactor itself was a potential bomb of far greater magnitude than any which might conceivably be used against it. In protecting the outside world and the plant's workers from the explosive potential of the reactor and the radiation in its core, the plant's designers had automatically protected the reactor from its enemies.

No, Lester acknowledged to himself, one could not attack the reactor itself, not directly. But if he was right—if the conduit Hinkley had shown him did indeed run through the middle of the shelf on which he sat—he could attack its heart. Its hearts, he corrected himself. For the reactor had three: three enormous core-coolant pumps which circulated through it the immense volume of liquid sodium required to keep the fires of the reactor core in check. If that coolant ceased to circulate for even a few seconds, the reactor would self-destruct.

With studied casualness, Lester poked about in his lunch pail, found a cookie, and stuffed it into his mouth. Rummaging again, he palmed the penknife and dropped his hand behind the brickwork. Cautiously, telling himself not to hope, he probed. And probed farther. The tip of his knife pinged against metal.

After reinserting the brick and pocketing his handkerchief, Lester ate the rest of his lunch with both hands in plain view. He was thinking of Christmas.

11

ALTHOUGH HE HAD TRIED several times, Hanson had never been able to precisely date the beginning of his conversion. The closest he could come was a general period, a season: the winter of his second year at Sand Beach.

For his doubts about the ultimate safety of the Sand Beach reactor had dawned slowly, bearing no resemblance whatsoever to the flashy drama of a religious revelation. They had emerged as the consequence of a gradual erosion of preconceptions, without even, in their early stages, pushing forward into his consciousness.

It occurred to him that the term "conversion" was curiously appropriate. For there was much in the relationship between nuclear reactor and Operations Supervisor to suggest the bond between a priest and the godhead he served. The analogy could even be extended. For just as the world's major religions each had a book of revelations in which the godhead revealed himself, but never all of himself, so the texts of nuclear physics set forth all that was known about nuclear-reactor dynamics—but, to date at least, not nearly all there was to know.

A large breeder reactor such as Sand Beach, like a god reserving certain knowledge of himself to himself, held mysteries and worked in ways no mortal entirely divined. Take the power surges, Hanson thought: phenomena familiar to every reactor operator, yet fully understood by none. With all systems stable, no instrument manipulated, not a single control rod moved, a reactor would suddenly, unpredictably, like a restless giant flexing its muscles, put out a power pulse. When the pulses were relatively mild, they could be, and were, controlled routinely. But routine measures did not always suffice at Sand Beach. Four times in three years, the reactor had generated power surges of such intensity that their suppression had required the emergency measure of scramming the reactor. Strong or weak, such pulses were neither predictable nor explicable. And there were many other such curious phenomena, similarly ill-understood processes whose labeling—"neutron flux," or "resonance"—disguised fundamental ignorance.

But the latter phenomena did not trouble him. Ill-understood as they were, they were nonetheless controllable. Displaying recognizable symptoms, they, like certain diseases, could be successfully treated symptomatically.

Raising his hand, Hanson pulled at his cheeks. He was little inclined to philosophizing, and found himself faintly surprised at the abstract turn his thoughts had taken. Yet the religious metaphor, though unbidden, did seem to capture the essence of his dilemma. It would be absurd, of course, to think of the Sand Beach reactor—a mere machine, after all—as malevolent, much less as willfully so. In ministering to it, whatever its omnipotent potential for destruction, he was scarcely serving a deity, whether god or devil. Yet, irrefutably, there was an element of Manichaeism in it all. And in deciding that the reactor should be shut down, he was guilty of subscribing to that heresy.

"Jesus!" Paul voiced the exclamation aloud. Enough was enough. Shoving his chair away from the desk, he rose, walked through the silent, empty house to the kitchen, and mixed himself a highball. He had a decision to make. A hard-headed decision that would drastically affect his entire life. Drifting off into analogical inanities wasn't going to help him make it.

Drink in hand, he returned to his study, determined to confront the real issue, one that had nothing whatsoever to do with gods, devils, priests, or heresies: whether or not to write a letter to the chairman of the Nuclear Regulatory Commission.

It was necessary to decide before Sherry and Katie returned from their pre-Christmas visit to Sherry's mother. For once they were back, the chance to reflect would be gone. It was not the sort of decision that lent itself to committee vote, even when the only members of the committee were his own wife and daughter.

He did not want to write the letter. Yet for almost three weeks now, ever since he had received the reply from Consolidated Power's President, Earl Stafford, he had secretly known that he must.

That intuitive knowledge had dogged him, shadowing each day, a bleak duty distant on the horizon but nonetheless inescapable, borne inevitably toward him by the steady winds of conscience. It would, he recognized, destroy his scarcely launched career as surely and irreparably as a torpedo circling back on the very ship that had fired it. The irony was that that was probably all it would accomplish—the chances of its finding its intended mark were slim.

Even though he knew the letter's contents almost by heart, he nevertheless pulled out the top drawer of his desk and extracted Stafford's response to his fears. In writing the President of Consolidated Power, he had risked nothing. His concern might even be counted as a plus—a sign of dedication. So long as you kept it in the Family and struck a properly respectful tone, you were permitted, without penalty, to quietly yell and scream. Until, that is, you were instructed, with polite and euphemistic firmness, to shut up. If you persisted . . . well, you had been warned.

But the consequences of ill-advised persistence were nothing compared to the penalty for going outside the Company. The Family would protect its own, so long as one remained loyal. But to go outside, to expose the Family to public scrutiny, to turn against your own kind—that was blasphemous treason. Traitors forfeited all claims to the milk of corporate kindness. They must expect to be, and were, summarily fired. And their names passed along, lest some other worthy Family benightedly take them in.

Such mutual self-protection required nothing so crudely illegal as a blacklist. In the small, incestuous world of nuclear physics, it was admirably accomplished by word of mouth alone. It all boiled down to a few phone calls.

That recognition evoked from Hanson a faint grimace as he reflected on how quickly his career would evaporate in the course of a few such calls. Then he shrugged and focused his attention on Stafford's letter.

"Dear Mr. Hanson," he read:

I wish, first of all, to express my own personal, as well as the Company's, appreciation for your concern about the ultimate safety of the Sand Beach nuclear installation. If all physicists in your position displayed a similar dedication, there is no question in my mind that the already outstanding safety record achieved by commercial nuclear generating stations would be further enhanced.

But let me turn to the specific matters raised in your letter, for they are indeed important; so important that they must, and should, occupy the thoughts of all those who are involved, in whatever capacity, with nuclear-generated power.

First of all, concerning the hypothetical possibility of the meltdown-crashdown sequence to which you allude. As I indicated earlier, your concern over potential health hazards to the public is quite proper. However, it does seem to me that the SAS and Venus core disassembly analysis codes, with which you are familiar, represent convincing evidence that the coherent fuel motion required to impart to such a highly improbable event explosive potential is most unlikely. Nevertheless, I would, it goes without saying, appreciate learning any further thoughts you might have on this matter.

With regard to your concern over *e*-folding time . . .

Hanson tossed the letter to the desk top in disgust. On it went, all five pages of it, polite and totally beside the point. At no point did Stafford (or, more probably, the P.R. man who had written it for him) address the real issue he had raised.

He wasn't concerned with the small amounts of fuel movement considered in the design-basis accidents and analyzed using the SAS and Venus computer codes. For that type of minor meltdown, the codes probably were accurate. But the perturbation-reactivity theory on which the Venus disassembly code was based held only for such small movements of fuel materials. What he feared was massive fuel motion following an initial meltdown, an autocatalytic compression or implosion of core materials that would amplify the primary disassembly, possibly creating a true nuclear explosion. For that was what had the capacity to breach the reactor vessel, and even the containment dome itself. The analysis of such potentially explosive fuel-motion configurations was totally beyond the capabilities of the Venus code. He felt certain that Stafford knew this perfectly well, and had simply chosen to ignore it.

His fresh anger at Stafford's slick evasiveness prodded him into a decision. Swiveling his chair away from the desk, he drew himself up to the typewriter table, inserted a sheet of paper, and began to type:

Mr. Calman Richards, Chairman
United States Nuclear Regulatory Commission . . .

12

IN ORDER TO INSURE ABSOLUTE PRIVACY, Ken Dirk had called
Nolan Kline, the officer in charge of Perimeter Security, to his
office. He held a trump, but wasn't sure how to play it. He
hoped Kline could help him decide.

More than a year before, backed and financed by his union,
Cuthright had gone to court alleging harassment, and had won
an injunction. Cuthright had contended that Consolidated
Power was attempting to coerce his resignation by subjecting
him to daily body searches. He had further alleged that Security Control officers conducted these searches with calculated
brutality, including painful and humiliating explorations of his
anal orifice and large intestine which had, on more than one
occasion, resulted in subsequent hemorrhaging.

Consolidated Power had defended itself on the following
grounds: all employees at its nuclear plants were subject to
body searches, a condition of employment was signing a
release permitting such searches, Cuthright had signed such a
release, and the alleged brutality was a figment of Cuthright's
inflamed imagination.

The Company's defense was rejected. Finding in favor of
the plaintiff, the Court ordered that the body searches to
which Cuthright was subjected thenceforth conform in fre-
quency and form to the norm for all employees at the Sand
Beach Nuclear Plant. In practical terms, that ruling meant an
over-outer-clothing frisk no more often than once a month.

The Court did make one exception: If Consolidated Power
could show probable and reasonable cause, it could subject
Cuthright to a strip-and-probe search. The judge's wording of
this qualification made it clear that such a search would be
expected to produce results. In essence, Dirk reflected, the
Company had been granted the right to do one additional strip
search on Cuthright. If they found something, he was out; if
they didn't, that was to be the end of it.

70

It was the timing of the search which Dirk wanted to discuss with Nolan Kline. When the trump was played, he had resolved, it must take the trick.

"I think he may be up to something, sir," Kline said.

Even as he catalogued the implications of Kline's comment, Dirk smiled at his subordinate's respectful, deliberate distancing. The two other chiefs of Perimeter Security viewed Kline as Dirk's pet, scorned him as a college jerk who, as the saying went, had his nose so far up the boss's ass you could only see his toes wiggle. For what but brown-nosing could explain Kline's permanent assignment to the coveted nine-to-five daytime shift? Only Dirk himself knew the real reason for the unusual and abrasive arrangement. He regarded Kline as the brightest of the three Perimeter Security officers, and Cuthright as the greatest threat to Plant security. As a hardship case, Cuthright worked only the preferred nine-to-five shift. To rotate Perimeter Security Chiefs while Cuthright worked the same shift month after month would inevitably play into Cuthright's hands. Man-to-man defense—that was Dirk's philosophy. So he had put Kline on Cuthright. And the comment Kline had just made provided all the justification he needed.

"You think he may be up to something?"

"Yes, sir."

"Go on."

Kline moved uneasily. "I'm not sure, of course," he said.

"Just tell me about it, okay?"

Kline nodded, squirmed again in his chair, and tried to sort out his thoughts. Dirk made him nervous. Not Dirk exactly, but Dirk's preoccupation with this Cuthright.

"Nail him!" Everything Dirk said transmitted that message. It was getting to the point where he couldn't determine whether what he saw was reality or merely a projection of Dirk's conviction that Cuthright was a crazy.

With some reluctance, he found himself compelled to acknowledge the possibility of a third explanation. His growing suspiciousness could result, quite simply, from guilt. For, until the Court put an end to it, he had been the instrument of Dirk's calculated policy of harassment. If the poor son of a bitch wasn't a threat, then he, Nolan Kline, in adding to the man's misery, had stooped pretty low.

"Well?" Dirk demanded.

Caught off balance in the midst of his speculations, Kline blurted out, "He seems *happy,* sir." As the bald absurdity of his words registered, he felt his face flush. Nonetheless, despite the clumsy, silly-sounding way he had put it, that was the whole thing in a nutshell. There was something strange, unsettling, even menacing about a man as miserable as Cuthright being happy.

Dirk thought so, too. Compressing his lips, he rocked back in his chair, folded his arms stolidly across his chest, and studied his perceptive subordinate. "Since when?" he asked.

"I'm not sure," Kline admitted. The seriousness with which Dirk had greeted his comment had banished his embarrassment. "A month, maybe. I didn't really notice it, couldn't put a finger on whatever was different about him, until the second time he smiled."

Dirk experienced two emotions simultaneously: an absolute certainty that Cuthright had discovered a means to sabotage the Plant, and a stomach-knotting premonition that he would succeed. That double whammy of insight and dread was no unfamiliar feeling. He knew it all too well from high-stakes poker, and hated it. It came toward the end of a big hand, when you were in deep and headed deeper, pushing, convinced of a lock, milking the sucker across the table, riding high. And then, all of a sudden, with one casual "Raise you back" too many, with a curious tic around the lips, or, as often as not, with no overt, consciously noted clue at all, an intuition that the other guy was the one with the lock, that he was the one pushing, that you were the sucker being milked.

Working to kill the flash of bitter hopelessness, Dirk reminded himself that this wasn't poker—in this game, the rules were different. Still, the image of Cuthright smiling was unnerving. It had been more than two years now since the man had been transferred from the Green Valley Plant to Sand

72

Beach, a transfer engineered in the vain hope that Cuthright might quit rather than be uprooted, parted from his cracker family and red-neck cronies. In the course of those two years, Dirk calculated, he had spent a hundred hours watching the man, occasionally face to face but mainly on the closed-circuit monitors. And in all that time, he had never witnessed Cuthright's thin, tight lips form a smile.

"What kind of smile?" he asked, returning his attention to Kline.

"Sure as hell not for me," Kline said. He paused, thinking back, and tried to work up a picture. Yes, he thought, the image growing more precise, that was it, just how he had looked, the expression exactly the same both times.

"It was a private smile," he said. "Like in a daydream." He studied the mental image some more. "Not friendly or amused. Not humorous. Not voluntary, either." He hesitated, trying to get the full flavor of Cuthright's expression. "Self-satisfied. Like he had something special that pleased him, and was looking at it, and just couldn't help smiling at the thought of it." Kline slumped back, surprised at how drained the effort had left him. Dirk swam in his blurred vision. Annoyed, blinking repeatedly, he struggled to refocus his eyes.

Dirk didn't even notice his subordinate's curious grimaces. For, as Kline spoke, his eyes, too, had turned inward. That Cuthright had made some malevolent discovery was, to Dirk, a totally foregone conclusion, yet the evidence was too insubstantial for action. The shadow of a sardonic, unconscious smile played for a moment across his own lips as he reflected on the Company's response to any letter he might write from Kline's report. He visualized the answering memo:

To: Kenneth Dirk, Chief, Security Control
Re: Your recent communication regarding Rad Protection Technician Lester Cuthright

Regret to inform you that two smiles are insufficient justification for discharge of said employee.

Then suspension, he thought. But that notion, too, quickly

succumbed to common sense. Abandoning such wish-fulfilling fantasies, he turned his attention to Kline. They would have to get some sort of evidence, something more solid than two goddamned smiles. They would have to play their trump.

"I'll tighten up inside," he told Kline. "Put him under closer surveillance. Try to figure out what he's up to."

Kline nodded. His own instructions, he knew, were coming.

"We've got that one strip search left," Dirk continued. "I want you to use it the next time you catch the bastard with that smile."

It was an off chance at best, Kline acknowledged, certain that Dirk shared his assessment. But it was all they had.

When Dirk remained silent, Kline rose, glanced again at his boss, and found him staring moodily at the plexiglass-shielded scram button on the corner of his desk. Turning away, he walked out of the office.

13

CALMAN RICHARDS had been in line for the chairmanship of the Nuclear Regulatory Commission for a full ten years before it was finally offered to him. By age forty-three he had risen to the staff position of Assistant to the Chairman. So, when John Harvey became ill and resigned, he was eligible to succeed him. If he had been appointed then, he would have been the youngest chairman in the Commission's history—but he was passed over. Four years later, when Harvey's successor got drunk and drove into a tree, he was passed over again. Six more years went by before circumstances granted him a third chance. That time he made it. And by that time he had come to understand why he hadn't made it earlier. His quick temper and raised, intimidating voice were assets that had helped propel him up through the ranks in the early stages of his career, but they became liabilities when the question of his fitness for Chairman arose.

Low profile. Dignity. Such were the two hallowed precepts of the NRC. Preserving the former while enhancing the latter was the primary function of any Commission Chairman. Obviously, a hothead wouldn't do. They had waited for him to mellow.

He hadn't. But, after the second opportunity had come and gone, he had recognized the necessity of conveying the impression that he had. He had acted convincingly, in the process learning much about self-discipline. Three years ago, the leading role he had rehearsed for so long had finally been granted him.

Thus, when Richards received Hanson's letter, he was well equipped by long practice to restrain himself from hasty, foolish action.

What especially infuriated him was that he would have to pretend cordiality, make a credible pretense of investigating—in short, try to placate a traitorous bastard who should be summarily dismissed. And somehow, while accomplishing all this, contrive to keep the matter from coming to the attention of the press.

Never for an instant did he entertain the slightest notion that Hanson's allegations might have merit. For Hanson's letter contained the hateful trigger words of all anti-nuclear agitation: "crashdown," "fuel motion," "secondary runaway," "autocatalysis," "violent disassembly." Richards could no more control his instant anger at the sight of those insufferable symbols than a Pavlovian hound could refuse to drool at the ring of its dinner bell. Eighteen years of service in the Commission had immutably conditioned him to loathe those terms, and to regard as an enemy every person who didn't smile deprecatingly when he used them.

Richards punched the intercom and instructed his secretary to give him thirty minutes without interruptions. Then, pushing down at the arms of his chair, he hoisted himself up. The effort that action required evoked, as usual, a fleeting awareness of his bulk, and an equally idle resolution to lose some weight. Two hundred and ten pounds on a five-foot-seven-inch frame was definitely stretching the credible limits of "stout." If he wasn't careful, he'd end up a fat man, and he hated fat men almost as much as he hated troublemakers like Hanson.

On his feet, Richards took a turn around his office; he always thought best while pacing. The spacious office suite which the comfortable indulgence of this predilection required was a minor but nonetheless soul-satisfying consequence of his elevation to Chairman.

Essentially, he reflected, pausing on his second circumnavigation to rest his arms on the back of his desk chair, it boiled down to containment. Like a person infected with a highly contagious disease, Hanson must be quarantined, his illness prevented from spreading. At the thought of the press, the most probable carrier, Richards switched metaphors. The script had all the earmarks of a best-seller. All the elements of a plot with proven popular appeal were there: Hanson, the hero, screaming doomsday; the Nuclear Regulatory Commission, villainous as always in such scenarios, trying to muzzle him; and, rounding out the cast of stock characters, the "innocent public," a defenseless maiden caught in the middle, confused, but rooting, of course, for the hero.

Obviously, Richards observed to himself, resuming his perambulation around the room, it was necessary to proceed with caution. Especially in view of the fact that this Hanson was a physicist—worse yet, the Operations Supervisor at Sand Beach.

That was the problem in a nutshell: Hanson's position. If he were just one more ignorant fool waving a sign, no one would notice; nor would his allegations about the safety hazards at Sand Beach carry much weight coming from the mouth of one of the professional gadflies of the nuclear-power industry. Such protestations were expected from these career agitators, and were discounted: after all, inventing scary fairy tales was their way of earning a living. But coming from a well-credentialed nuclear physicist—a man responsible for operating the very installation he was criticizing, a man who was clearly jeopardizing his entire career by making those charges —that was something else. That was, Richards reluctantly acknowledged, almost unheard of. Since the news media operated according to the premise that man-bites-dog was newsworthy, they would undoubtedly make a big deal out of a physicist biting the hand that had so generously fed him.

Thus, Richards resolved, the matter of highest priority was to keep Hanson away from the media. The fact that the son of a bitch had written to him instead of to some muckraking columnist was one mark in his favor, and provided grounds for optimism. He obviously didn't want to make a stink just for the sake of being a skunk. If Hanson could be placated, he would probably shut up, and the whole matter would die quietly.

Ruminations resolved, Richards strode to his desk and buzzed his secretary. "Ring up Earl Stafford for me," he told her. "Consolidated Power in New York."

"I don't know a damned thing about the bastard, Cal," Earl Stafford commented into the telephone. "He wrote me the same letter, from what you've said, but I never dreamed he'd keep at it."

Stafford listened for a moment, grunted agreement, and then continued. "I've gotten a couple of letters like that every year since I made President. Nothing's ever come of any of them. They're always written by new boys, just like Hanson. They work for two or three years, experience a few power surges, and get spooked. So they write me looking for reassurance, Big Daddy telling them it's okay. I write back—we've got a really beautiful form letter—and that's the end of it. The first few times I overreacted—canned them. I didn't realize then it was a pattern. Now I don't even put it in their files. You can understand—"

Wincing at the volume of Richards's interruption, Stafford listened to the remainder of the man's diatribe holding the receiver a full inch away from his ear.

"Yes," he said, tentatively pressing the receiver back against his head. "Of course. I understand that this is a different story. *Entirely* different," he quickly amended, repeating Richards's characterization, lest the man shout a correction. "And I agree with your assessment of the media danger."

This time Richards's response grew louder gradually. Stafford avoided pain by a steady distancing of ear and receiver.

"Let me make a suggestion," Stafford commented mildly when Richards ran out of steam. Twice burned, he was twice wary. As he spoke, he kept a good half inch of sound-deadening air between his head and the phone's earpiece. "I'll get hold of the plant manager and get the lowdown on this Hanson. Find out whether he's a kook, just stupid, or what. Then I'll call you back and we can decide how to proceed, okay?"

There was a pause, during which Stafford listened intently. "Right, Cal. I know that. Of course I appreciate your concern. I'll get back to you tomorrow." He heard a skeptical grunt, and then the connection was broken.

Stafford gave himself a few moments to allow the ringing in his ears to subside. Then, preferring to get it over with, he rang his secretary and instructed her to get Ron Claton at Sand Beach on the line. While she was putting the call through, he walked across the room, slid back the panels of the hidden bar, and mixed himself a drink. Richards could be a real pain in the ass.

14

FOR TWO DAYS—ever since Tuesday morning, when Cuthright had again smiled, and thereby forced his carefully hoarded trump—Dirk had been mad. Kline had called from the gate to announce that the search was underway; a half-hour later, he had shown up in person to announce its failure.

Dirk's foul mood had played no favorites, so when he barked, "What is it?" into the intercom, the voice of Jill, his secretary, was timid.

"The report just arrived, sir," she murmured. Her trepidation rendered the message scarcely audible.

"What?" Dirk demanded. "Speak up, for Christ's sake. What report?" His tone overrode his command. Jill's reply came in a whisper.

"The Cuthright report, sir." After a moment, hesitantly, she added, "You instructed me to inform you the moment—"

"Bring it in," Dirk interrupted.

In the report lay the one remaining hope of salvaging something from the debacle. Kline said they had found nothing, but he had been looking for the obvious: a weapon, a bomb, some clearly criminal tool. He might have overlooked a more subtle sign.

A presence impinged on his awareness, and he glanced up. Jill was standing rigidly before his desk. Like one forced against her will to extend a bone to a vicious dog, she offered the report tremulously, at arm's length. She was so obviously fearful, so blatantly scared of being snapped at, that Dirk impulsively lunged forward across his desk, roaring a vicious snarl. She screamed. He laughed—it was good therapy. Jill watched him warily from the spot several feet away where her terrified leap had planted her.

"Have I really been such a bastard lately?" he said.

Perceiving it had been a joke, his secretary managed a wan

80

smile. "Yes, sir. I'm afraid you have." The report, frail armor, was clasped to her equally insubstantial breasts.

Why, Dirk reflected idly, couldn't he have gotten a secretary with a decent ass and some real tits, instead of this skinny mouse? A real ball breaker, like that broad in Cliff's office over at Big Rock? A beanpole for a secretary and Cuthright too, he thought; what a crock.

"Give me half an hour," he said, holding out his hand for the report, which the mouse was still holding against her chest. "Don't put any calls through unless it's urgent."

"Yes, sir." Jill smiled. Her relief at his restored cordiality was as obvious as her earlier fear.

Dirk nodded a dismissal and forgot her, his thoughts already focused on the report. It compromised a comprehensive inventory of Cuthright's clothing and personal effects, along with a detailed laboratory analysis.

STRIP-SEARCH INVENTORY AND REPORT
SUBJECT: LESTER CUTHRIGHT
POSITION: RADIATION PROTECTION TECHNICIAN

General. Subject was searched at the order of Nolan Kline, Chief, Perimeter Security Control, on the morning of December 10th after presenting himself to Gate Security preliminary to Plant entry. Subject made no active resistance to the search procedure. Subject made no voluntary comments in the course of the search, speaking only in response to direct questions. Upon preliminary negative search results, subject was issued interim clothing, food in his lunch pail was returned to him in a paper bag, and he was allowed to enter the plant.

Garments.   Subject was wearing garments as follows:
blue dacron windbreaker jacket
plaid flannel outer shirt
white cotton undershirt
gray denim trousers
black leather belt with toggle buckle
boxer undershorts, cotton
leather work boots
white cotton socks

Personal Effects.   Personal effects in possession of subject, and location, follow:

Effect	Location
key ring: four keys, two auto, two house	jacket, right-hand pocket, outer side
tin of Old Durham chewing tobacco	jacket, left-hand pocket, outer side
black felt-tip pen	shirt, left-hand breast pocket
Timex wristwatch, steel band	left wrist
assorted loose change, $0.78 total	trousers, right-hand pocket
assorted loose change, $0.35 total	trousers, left-hand pocket
red bandanna handkerchief	trousers, right-hand hip pocket
billfold—inventory as follows:	trousers, left-hand hip pocket

a) cash: 2 fives, 4 ones
b) social security card, #525-90-5988
c) Consolidated Power employee-identification card
d) driver's license
e) Shell Oil Company credit card
f) automobile-registration card
g) automobile certificate-of-insurance card
h) Blue Cross-Blue Shield health-insurance card
i) Selective Service registration card
j) paper scrap with telephone number (Number identified as unlisted home phone of physician who treats subject's son)

| two-bladed penknife | lunch pail |

Laboratory Analysis. Chemical analysis of residual material and debris follows:

Substance	Location
tobacco particles	jacket, left-hand pocket
tobacco particles	shirt, left-hand breast pocket
chewing-gum fragments	jacket, right-hand pocket
miscellaneous food particles	jacket, left-hand pocket
stain, lubricating oil two centimeters diameter	jacket, left-side, mid-chest
whitish dust, composition compatible with mortar traces	bottom lining of right-hand hip pocket
whitish dust, as above	penknife, in grease of hinge mechanism
miscellaneous food particles and fragments	lunch pail

Dirk read through the report three times before finally acknowledging defeat.

Nothing. Not a goddamned thing.

15

LESTER WENT BACK TO HIS ROOTS, back to Tennessee, to get the explosive he needed. For five weeks after finally working the brick loose, he had waited impatiently for Christmas. Every year at that time, he took two of his annual three-weeks' vacation time and made a pilgrimage back home, carrying with him, like worthless but undiscardable family heirlooms, his Valium-tranquilized son and liquor-besotted wife.

Those annual fourteen days (actually only twelve after the driving time) were the only true freedom Lester knew from one year to the next. There were enough kin-folk on both sides of the family to care for a dozen Erics and Rachels. So he dumped them on the care of others without compunction, and devoted himself to forgetting.

He followed a rigid routine, a satisfying tradition, established even before his forced relocation to Sand Beach and scrupulously adhered to in the two vacations since. The first night he spent with his folks. The second he got blind drunk and had to be carried home. The third he spent with a whore. The remaining nine days and nights he passed with kin and cronies, returning to his folks' place only late in the evening, when he knew Rachel and Eric would be asleep.

This time he spent the first night as usual. But he renounced the drunk and the whore.

Instead, for six days and nights in succession, he worked the bars, finding the boys he knew from the good old days, now aged, like himself, to dry manhood, buying a round, chewing the fat, and finally, always, mentioning what he wanted.

Spreading the word around like that caused him no concern whatsoever: these were his kind. When they spoke to others, as they would, and as he intended that they should, his name would not come up. He was throwing pebbles into a score of ponds. Each toss would start ripples spreading outward in ever-widening circles. Eventually, he knew with absolute, unquestioning certainty, a name would come back to him.

A little after eight P.M. on the night of the sixth day, his faith was rewarded. He was nursing a beer in the Green Spot when Harvey Caslin came in, took the bar stool next to his, and ordered a draft beer. They talked about the hound Harvey had bought last year that wasn't working out. When both beers were gone, they walked out of the bar together and got into Harvey's mud-spattered six-year-old pickup.

"His name's Ralph Willard," Harvey said as he swung the truck onto the two-lane blacktop and headed toward Murphysburg. "Know him?"

Lester shook his head.

"He's the fellow that married Flo Corey the year after you got transferred." Harvey glanced over, and this time Lester nodded. "Works at the gasket plant in Murphysburg," Harvey added. "His pa's got a farm up by Marion, but it ain't much, so when Willie got hitched he didn't have no choice but the factory."

Lester nodded again, showing he was satisfied.

"Claims he knows a sergeant—ex-sergeant," Harvey amended, "that used to have it. Long time ago, though. Right after Vietnam. Seems the guy got court-martialed and figured if he was gonna get screwed outa his benefits, he'd take something with him to help even things out. Willie figures even if he's sold what he had, he might be able to get hold of some more."

Caslin interrupted his monologue to peer ahead, letting the truck slow. After a moment he made a satisfied grunt, braked, then turned right onto a nondescript dirt road. The truck banged and skittered on the washboard surface.

"Willie was a private, lived in the same trailer court. They ain't seen each other for four, maybe five years, but Willie had an old address, down in Jackson. Took the day off to drive down there. Figure he oughta be back by now."

"Mighty white of him, doin' that," Lester allowed.

"Willie's a good boy," Harvey commented after a moment.

85

They drove on in silence for several minutes. Then, coming out of a dogleg, Harvey pointed to some lights up ahead to the left. "That's his place," he said.

As the pickup swung into the dirt driveway, Caslin's eyes flicked over Lester's face, then back to the road. "It's gonna cost you," he said. "From what Willie says, this fellow ain't in business for fun."

Lester made a single, sharp nod. He wasn't expecting, or accepting, any charity.

16

EVEN THOUGH HE KNEW IT WAS CORNY—maybe not as corny as renting a billboard and a sign painter, or hiring a plane to do skywriting, but corny—Paul did it anyway.

On the drive back from the airport, he was careful to keep the cat in the bag, dropping no clues. Sherry enthused about her visit, about how Katie had charmed everyone, about aunts, uncles, nephews, and nieces. All he had to do to keep her unsuspecting was pretend an interest in the gossip.

When he turned onto the sweeping, snow-covered drive that brought the house into view, Sherry became sentimental. "It's good to be home," she said, nestling up against him. "Good to be back again with you."

"I'll get the bags in a minute." He smiled. "Let's go on in first." He carried Katie from the car to the porch, shifting her to his left arm while he unlocked the door. "Go ahead," he told Sherry.

Her reaction was all he could have hoped for: shock, incredulity, delight. For Katie, it took a bit of getting used to. "What's Daddy done to the house?" she asked doubtfully. Though still in his arms, she looked to Sherry for an answer.

"He's decorated it for us." Sherry laughed. "To welcome us back."

"That's one way to describe it, I guess." Paul grinned. "Actually, I think 'festooned' comes closer to the mark."

The living room was a mad carnival of crepe-paper streamers, multicolored balloons, winking strings of Christmas lights, holly, tinsel, candy sticks, and paper angels. Suspended from the ceiling, a giant banner running the length of the room proclaimed WELCOME HOME SHERRY AND KATIE! Overall, it

87

reminded Paul of the efforts of a junior-high-school decorating committee, raised to the tenth power, the sort of thing such a committee might achieve given unlimited time, abundant funds, and manic zeal.

"I like it," Katie announced.

"You're a sweet idiot," Sherry told him later that evening as they sat together on the sofa beneath a festive canopy of crepe-paper ribbons. But her attempt to rekindle their earlier spontaneous joy was without success. With Katie asleep in bed, the house grown quiet, and the hour late, the magic was wearing away.

The trouble with this sort of thing, Paul thought, his arm about Sherry's shoulder, was that you knew it had to come down. Routine day-to-day living simply could not be conducted amid such spangled clutter. The recognition that high points of laughter and delight could not be sustained saddened him. It was the same with Christmas trees, he reflected, gazing at the small Blue Spruce before the picture window. They had driven to one of the outlying tree farms and cut it down themselves, savoring its scent all the way home. Then, together as a family, they had decorated it while Christmas carols played softly in the background. It, too, would eventually have to come down. He thought of his job: another nice thing in his life that would soon be gone.

"I wrote the letter," he said.

Sherry looked up, meeting and holding his eyes. "To the NRC?" she asked.

They had talked through the matter weeks before, after he had received the evasive reply from Stafford—the matter of whether or not to carry it further. It had to be his decision, Sherry had said, and he had not disagreed. She would accept it, whichever way it went. "I want you to know that," she had told him after the jokes about selling apples and taking in laundry were all done with. "Whatever you decide, that's what I want too."

He became aware of Sherry's tense stiffness under his

hand, and realized she was still waiting for his reply. "Yes," he said. "To the NRC."

Turning her lips against his neck, she kissed him softly, lovingly. "That was a brave thing to do," she murmured. "I'm proud to be married to a brave man."

17

IN HIS BASEMENT WORKROOM, Cuthright lifted the nondescript silver-gray toolbox from a shelf by the door and set it in the center of the cleared workbench. Hooking up a three-legged stool with his foot, he sat down, crossed his arms across his chest, and regarded the box with glittering eyes, as pridefully possessive as a vain woman before her jewelry chest. Though he had been back from vacation for over a week, this was his first opportunity to study his newly acquired treasures at length, the first chance he'd had to sit down undisturbed and actually begin to plan exactly how he would do it.

After a few moments of self-satisfied contemplation, he unclasped his arms, leaned forward, and began to manipulate the dial of the combination lock. 22-8-15. He mentally recited the numbers as he turned the dial: first two full circles right, then one and a bit more back to 8, then slowly to the right again, stopping with the pointer exactly centered on 15. In the night-deadened silence of the basement room, he fancied he heard the last tumbler falling and, with a slight tug, disengaged the lock. Setting it to one side, he freed the hasp from its ring and lifted the box's hinged lid. The contents that action exposed were, to him, quite as dazzling as diamonds.

The sight evoked the same smile on Cuthright's thin lips that, when Nolan Kline reported it, had scared Security Chief Kenneth Dirk into ordering the strip search. Methodically, the smile fading as he turned to business, Cuthright began to empty the box, placing its contents in a line from left to right on the scarred and pitted pine planks of the workbench.

First, almost reverently, he removed the block of C4 plastic explosive. Yesterday morning, before going to work, he had taken it to the branch post office two blocks away and had it weighed on the letter scale. The reason he gave himself was to see if he had been cheated; but there was a deeper, more compelling drive behind his rash and foolish act. Carrying about that deadly cube, lightly wrapped in tissue, gave him an exhilarating sense of power. Like an arsonist drawn back to witness the fire he himself had ignited, Lester, in passing the cube across the counter, was flaunting his superiority.

"Twenty-four ounces," the man had commented, handing the parcel back, "a shade over. But you'll have to wrap it better than that." Lester had nodded, given the man his thin smile, and walked away. He had paid for a pound and a half, and that's what he'd gotten.

Setting the one-and-a-half-by-eight-inch cube on the bench, Lester noticed the slight indentations his two-fingered grip had left. Just like Play-Doh, he thought, recollecting its feel and texture. A little bit harder, like compacted clay, but the same dull, off-white color as the stuff in one of those canisters he and Rachel had bought for Eric.

The memory, and the association, killed his good humor. In supermarkets and stores, the last months before Eric's birth, he had bought indiscriminately, impulsively, whenever he had found himself passing a toy counter. Eventually, by the time Rachel was due, the shelves of the special room they had decorated and furnished were overflowing. Filled with childish gimmickry, the nursery resembled a toy shop.

A few months after they had brought him home, when they could no longer deceive themselves that Eric would ever play with anything, they had spent an evening boxing the whole collection of shattered anticipations for a Christmas charity drive. In the beginning, they had toyed with each item before reluctantly consigning it to a box. That was when, with Rachel kneeling beside him, holding a tinkling stuffed pink rabbit, he had opened the Play-Doh.

But the protracted process had quickly become too painful, each toy or game a special constellation of happy play never to be. Rachel had begun to cry, then sob, as each image of the imaginary, longed-for child broke against the reality of the brain-damaged, flippered It. Lester had taken her from the room, comforted her, and finally, made sad, unenthusiastic love to her. When he was certain she slept, he had returned to Eric's room and crated the remainder of the toys with scarcely a glance. Then, in the dark of night, like a thief, he had stowed the boxes in the trunk of the car, so that Rachel would not have to see them the next morning.

It crossed his mind, grimly, that in the plastic's uncanny resemblance to that long-discarded play-clay there was a certain justice. It would be Eric's, as well as his own, revenge.

Assuaged by that notion, Lester returned to the business before him. From the toolbox he extracted the two electrical blasting caps, and placed them beside the plastic. The shiny silver of the caps complemented the hue of the explosive, seemed to suggest, encourage even, a mating. Lester took a T-bar from its hook on the pegboard behind the workbench and measured one of the cylinders. One and three-quarter inches long; just under one-quarter inch in diameter—not counting the wires, of course. He uncoiled the two detonating wires that disappeared into the base of the blasting cap, whipping them out along the bench. At least eight feet, he estimated. There was no need to determine the exact length: they were obviously long enough. Too long, in fact. They'd have to be cropped. He recoiled the wires and returned the cap to its place beside its partner.

The next item from the box was a cheap portable radio, hand-sized. Lester set it face down on the wooden bench top, prised open the lid with his thumbnail, and removed the battery. Holding it close to his face, he turned it until the side he wanted came up. Nine volts. The sergeant had told him each cap required one and a half volts, but it was better to be on the safe side. He pressed the battery back into its nest, snapped the cover in place, and set the radio alongside the blasting caps.

Only one item remained in the toolbox, a ragged-edged, coverless copy of the *Special Forces Handbook*. It had cost him two hundred dollars extra, but only temporarily. Ralph was holding the money. When he returned the handbook to the sergeant, Ralph would return the money to him—less the forty dollars the sergeant was charging him for the loan of the manual.

"Look," the sergeant had told him when he asked how to

put it all together, "I don't run a kindergarten." Lester could picture the fat bastard, looking down his nose. But he wanted the money, that was clear.

"Then it's no good," Lester had said, taking a chance. Actually, he would have gone through with the deal anyway. Getting the plastic was what counted, for it was the key to everything else. But he had known better than to say so. "I gotta know how to set it off."

The sergeant had stared at him for a while. Then, muttering obscenities, he left the room. When he returned a few moments later, he held the book.

"It's all in here," he said. "If you can read."

"I can read," Lester said, matching the sergeant's tone.

At that point, Ralph had broken in, cooling things down. The terms were set, and Lester got the instruction manual.

Now, with all the apparatus spread out before him, Lester turned to the first page and found the table of contents. "You want a diamond charge and a timer," the sergeant had commented cryptically. Lester looked up "diamond charge" first. There was both a written description and an illustration.

DIAMOND CHARGE. This charge can be used to cut hard or alloy steel cylindrical targets of any size that would conceivably be encountered. Dimensions are as follows: The long axis of the diamond charge should equal the circumference of the target, and the points should just touch on the far side. The short axis is equal to one-half the circumference. Thickness of the charge is 1/3 thickness of a block of C-3 or C-4. To prime the charge, both points of the short axis must be primed for simultaneous detonation. This can be accomplished electrically or by use of equal lengths of detonating cord, with a cap crimped on the end that is inserted into the charge. As detonation is initiated in each point of the diamond and moves toward the center, the detonating waves meet at the exact center of the charge, are deflected downward, and cut the shaft cleanly at that point. The diamond charge is more time consuming to construct, and requires both more care and more materials to prime. Transferring the charge dimensions to a template or cardboard or even cloth permits relatively easy charge construction (working directly on the target is extremely difficult). The completed wrapped charge is then transferred to the target and taped or tied in place, insuring that maximum close contact is achieved. The template technique should be used for the diamond charge.

DIAMOND CHARGE

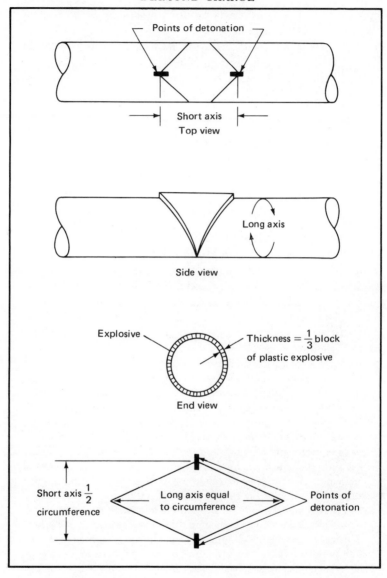

Points of detonation

Short axis
Top view

Long axis

Side view

Explosive

Thickness = $\frac{1}{3}$ block
of plastic explosive

End view

Short axis $\frac{1}{2}$
circumference

Long axis equal
to circumference

Points of
detonation

Lester read the description through three times, occasionally glancing from the printed text to the schematic drawing. His first reading was cautious, almost reluctant, for he had feared, even secretly expected, to find the project beyond his capabilities. Thus, he approached each sentence warily, steeling himself against the threat to his scheme posed by its unknown content. His second reading was slower still, word by silently mouthed word; he could not allow himself to believe, without rechecking, that it could be so simple. The third time he read the explanation he smiled.

"Timer," he muttered to himself. He was eager now, the book no longer a potential enemy but a friend. It had been written, he realized, to help men just like himself—plain, average men who had something they wanted to blow up. On pages III-31 and III-32, he found what he needed.

As he read through the six-step procedure, Lester cupped his chin in the palm of his hand and pulled at his jowls. It was incredible. He was going to blow up Sand Beach with ten cents' worth of dried peas.

DRIED SEED TIMER

A time delay device for electrical firing circuits can be made using the principle of expansion of dried seeds.

MATERIAL REQUIRED:

Dried peas, beans or other dehydrated seeds
Wide mouth glass jar with nonmetal cap
Two screws or bolts   Thin metal plate
Hand drill   Screwdriver

PROCEDURE:

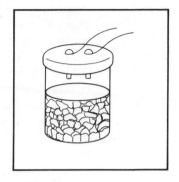

1. Determine the rate of rise of the dried seeds selected. This is necessary to determine delay time of the timer.

a. Place a sample of the dried seeds in the jar and cover with water.

b. Measure the time it takes for the seeds to rise a given height. Most dried seeds increase 50% in 1 to 2 hours.

2. Cut a disc from thin metal plate. Disc should fit loosely inside the jar.

> NOTE: If metal is painted, rusty or otherwise coated, it must be scraped or sanded to obtain a clean metal surface.

3. Drill two holes in the cap of the jar about 2 inches apart. Diameter of holes should be such that screws or bolts will thread tightly into them. If the jar has a metal cap or no cap, a piece of wood or plastic (NOT METAL) can be used as a cover.

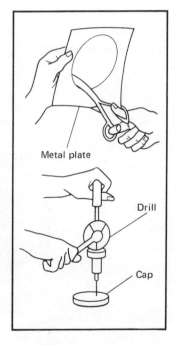

Metal plate

Drill

Cap

4. Turn the two screws or bolts through the holes in the cap. Bolts should extend about one in. (2 1/2 cm) into the jar.

> IMPORTANT: Both bolts must extend the same distance below the container cover.

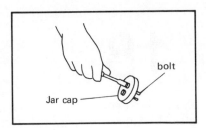

5. Pour dried seeds into the container. The level will depend upon the previously measured rise time and the desired delay.

6. Place the metal disc in the jar on top of the seeds.

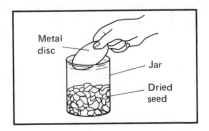

HOW TO USE:

1. Add just enough water to completely cover the seeds and place the cap on the jar.

2. Attach connecting wires from the firing circuit to the two screws on the cap.

Expansion of the seeds will raise the metal disc until it contacts the screws and closes the circuit.

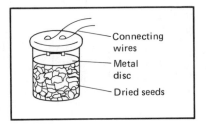

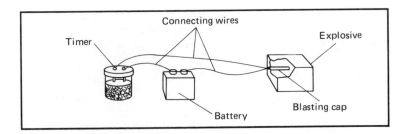

18

PAUL GOT HOME from the Plant a few minutes before six o'clock. Sherry met him at the door, holding an unopened letter. Almost three weeks had passed since he had written to the Nuclear Regulatory Commission, and for Sherry as well as for him, the waiting had become intolerable.

"So it finally came," he said. A glance at the envelope confirmed his intuition.

"I was going to call you at the Plant to let you know," Sherry said, "But then I decided that would just make you worry the rest of the day, so I didn't."

He nodded in approval. "Good. It would have made the afternoon a year."

"Aren't you going to open it?" Sherry demanded. She trailed him eagerly, a terrier tracking a bone, as he walked into the living room and headed toward the kitchen.

"After I make a drink," he temporized.

Katie was crouched before the television, intent on the afternoon replay of *Sesame Street*. He said, "Hi," and ruffled her hair, but she ignored him.

In the kitchen, he propped the letter against the side of the toaster while he mixed a generous Manhattan. The drink was a way of armoring himself, of girding his loins for news with a high quotient of potential disappointment. He had procrastinated in the same manner before, once after receiving the letter that would tell him whether or not he had passed his Ph.D. general examinations, another time with a letter which he knew held the editor's decision on the publication or rejection of a monograph on which he had lavished six months of labor.

"Do you want one?" he asked Sherry, dropping in ice cubes.

She shook her head. "Open it. I've been waiting all afternoon."

Grinning at her eager impatience, Paul picked up the envelope, tapped it against the counter top, and tore a strip from one end.

"Read it loud," Sherry beseeched as he unfolded the single sheet.

" 'Dear Dr. Hanson,' " he read. " 'This is to acknowledge your communication of 18 December in which you allege substantial safety hazards at the Sand Beach Nuclear Plant and request a formal hearing so as to detail and elaborate on such putative hazards. In our judgment, convening a formal hearing at this point would be precipitous. However, it does appear that a preliminary inquiry is in order. I propose to hold such an inquiry on January 13th. If this date is satisfactory, I would appreciate your phoning my secretary, who will provide you with the specific time and place, as well as clarify any other questions you may have.'

"It's signed, 'Sincerely, Calman Richards,' " Paul said, letting the letter fall to the counter top. He took a pull at his drink to mask his disappointment.

"It doesn't say a thing," Sherry cried. She was indignant. "He didn't respond to anything you said."

"Maybe he wants to wait for the inquiry. At least he's setting that up."

"Hell!" Sherry exclaimed. "That's just so he'll be covered. What an ass!"

Her vehement prejudice forced Paul to come to Richards's defense. Even though the man's failure to address the substance of his charges was disappointing, he could see the logic of it. Informed judgment demanded full information. In refusing to comment on the merit of his allegations, Richards was simply being cautious.

When he shared that rationalization with Sherry, she shrugged, unconvinced. "All right, then," she said, "so maybe he's not an ass. But I don't trust him."

Paul grinned. One thing was for sure—he had a wife who believed in fighting for her man.

19

IF ONE DIDN'T LOOK TOO CLOSELY, the scene in the living room could easily have been mistaken for that of a typical family watching after-dinner TV together. A closer glance, however, exposed discordant notes. The quiet, well-behaved child watching television with his parents was sightless and deformed, nodding not from sleepiness but from drugs. The plump but otherwise unexceptional housewife was revealed as unmistakably obese, and, just as clearly, intoxicated, the mug on the sofa armrest beside her filled not with coffee but with gin. And the thin, intense man apparently overwrought by the drama of the televised chase scene turned out, on closer inspection, to have his eyes turned inward, his electric rigidity stemming not from excitement but from suppressed rage.

Any other evening, Lester would have been happy at the rare semblance of domestic tranquility. Quiet, seemingly content, Eric was giving no trouble. And though Rachel was blasted, she wasn't stumbledown, out-of-control drunk. She had managed dinner, and had even made a stab at cleaning up afterward. But tonight wasn't just any other evening. Tonight he had planned the test. Rachel's failure to pass out on schedule and Eric's unusual wakefulness were both conspiring against him.

Though he had checked the time no more than five minutes before, he glanced again at his watch. Almost ten o'clock. He figured on at least two hours for the test. He'd be dead tired all day tomorrow if he didn't get started soon.

"I'm going to take Eric up," he said. Engrossed in the television drama, Rachel made an absent-minded, disinterested nod. He had decided to begin without waiting for her to go to bed. At this rate, she could be in front of the tube all night.

Eric made no protest when Lester lifted him from the oversized perambulator. Fifteen minutes later, the ritual of cleaning, diapering, and sedating completed, Lester returned to the living room.

"I'm gonna do some stuff in the workroom," he told Rachel.

"Mmm."

"See you in bed," he added.

"Mmm." Her eyes never left the television.

Turning away, he headed toward the door of the basement.

In order to get the proper dimensions for the diamond charge, Lester had bought a segment of five-inch-diameter PVC plumbing pipe. Now, standing before the workbench, he measured its circumference with a piece of string. According to the diagram in the *Special Forces Handbook,* this would give him the "long axis"—a term he translated to mean overall length—for the charge. He transferred these two points to an opened grocery sack, doubled the string over to locate the midpoint, and then, using the same doubled string, marked the end points for the diamond's width—"short axis," the book called it. Using a straight edge, he proceeded to connect all four points.

After scissoring away the excess paper, he picked up the paper diamond and wrapped it experimentally around the length of pipe, being careful to align the two short-axis points on top. The tips of the long axis met, exactly, on the underside of the pipe: he had his template.

Although the plastic explosive looked and felt like Play-Doh, it did not have Play-Doh's sweetish smell; in fact, it had no discernible odor whatsoever. Lester regarded it with distrust.

"Don't worry," the sergeant had told him, in a voice dripping with scornful condescension, when he had gingerly accepted the little package. "This is the real thing, military grade. You can hammer it, shoot at it, set fire to it. There ain't nothin gonna set if off 'cept them caps."

Half expecting an explosion, Lester raised the oblong cube above his head and then, in semi-suicidal frenzy, smashed it against the workbench. It went "squish" and became a blob. Grinning, Lester molded it with his hands, quickly achieving a ball. He then used Rachel's rolling pin, pilfered from the kitchen, to thin it down, cutting and trimming as he rolled. In less than fifteen minutes, the shape of the plastic and that of the template corresponded.

Grunting with satisfaction, Lester reached behind him for the stool and took a break. As he massaged the soreness out of his shoulders, all the while contemplating his handiwork, he smiled thinly. Things were moving along right well.

After perhaps a minute, he hiked the stool closer to the workbench. Leaning forward, he wrapped the diamond charge around the pipe, just as he had done earlier with the template, and secured the two tips of the long axis with a strip of tape. In a bind, he figured, he could just pinch the ends together and make the charge hold without the tape. Out of curiosity, he tried jiggling the blanket of explosive, and discovered that it held firm: the plastic had a slight adhesive quality.

This fact noted, Lester reached for the two nine-volt miniature light bulbs, wires preattached, which he had bought at a hobby shop. They were intended for model-railroad layouts. He planned to use them to test out his firing circuit.

It required only a few moments to affix the bulbs to the charge at each end of the short axis. The blasting caps, of course, would need no tape: they could simply be pushed into the plastic explosive like suppositories.

With the lights in place, wires dangling, Lester picked up the *Special Forces Handbook,* located the wiring diagram for the expansion-type timer he intended to employ, and studied it at length. This was the only part that was giving him trouble. If he felt he had grasped the principles involved, he would have been able to skip this trial run-through. But he was no electrician. He could replace a wall switch, matching the right wire to the right pole, but that was about it.

After a few minutes of study, Lester concluded that his problem stemmed from the fact that he had two blasting caps, and consequently four wires, instead of the one cap and two wires depicted in the sketch. He decided to splice the wires leading from the right-hand light bulb to the corresponding wires leading from the bulb on the left side of the charge. That would produce two "business" wires, which could be attached exactly as shown in the diagram.

Five minutes later, the cap of the slender olive jar having been drilled, sanded, and rigged with screws the night before, everything was connected. The light bulbs remained unlit. At least, Lester reflected, the way he had rigged, it wouldn't have blown him up. Whether it would work as intended remained to be seen.

He made a funnel of the sack's mouth and filled the olive jar to within an inch and a half of its lip with dried peas. Of course he would leave more room, and thus more time in which to get out of the area, when it came to the real thing. But now he just wanted to see if the contraption was going to work, without waiting up half the night to find out.

He shook the jar, making the contents settle, then added a few more peas by hand. Satisfied, he rose from the bench, walked out of his workroom to the basement clothes washer, rinsed the soap out of Rachel's measuring cup, and filled it with water.

Back on his three-legged perch, he tilted water into the jar until it just covered the peas. On top of that thin film he dropped the precut tin disk, and then, turning the jar rather than the top, tightened the lid. The ends of the two screws projecting into the jar were less than half an inch from the top of the metal plate. Supposedly, if he had done everything right, the plate would begin to rise until it contacted the two screws. That would complete the firing circuit, and the two bulbs would light up. When it came to the real thing, he thought, smiling again, that moment would be considerably more exciting.

Peering at the space between screws and plate, he fancied that the gap had already narrowed. He sat back, folded his arms across his chest, and stared fixedly at the two miniature light bulbs. It could happen at any moment.

"Lester!"

In the total oblivion of his transfixed concentration, that accusation—shrill, drawn-out, suspicious—exploded with the impact of a bomb. Like a furtive adolescent parent-trapped in mid-mastubatory ejaculation, Lester experienced an instant of hopeless horror even as, in animal reflex, he sprang from the stool, at bay, to face the enemy.

Rachel swayed against the door frame of the workroom, leering at him. With drunken prescience, she had divined his guilt.

"What you doin', Lester?" She grinned at him, half conspiratorial, half censorious, a sibling teetering between a desire to join in the naughty play and an equally strong impulse to run and tattle.

"Nothin'," Lester muttered. He took a step sideways, trying to block her view of the apparatus on the bench.

Rachel's grin broadened. She had obviously decided to stay and play. "You're up to somethin', Lester," she sniggered happily. "I can tell."

"I ain't doin nothin'," Lester stubbornly repeated.

But Rachel, having caught a glimpse of the strange paraphernalia on the workbench, rightly sensed that it was the secret.

"Whatcha makin'?" she asked coyly. When Lester didn't answer, she left the doorway and moved toward the bench to see for herself.

Lester let her pass. It wouldn't mean anything to her anyway.

Rachel was by the bench now, staring. "You puttin' a diaper on a pipe?" she asked. Her moment of lucidity was ebbing, leaving behind only foggy confusion. "With lights?"

Her eyes followed the wires to the battery, then on to the jar of peas. She shook her head as if to clear her vision.

"What *are* you doin', Lester?" she again demanded. But this time there was no suspicion, just whining befuddlement.

"Well, lookee there!" Rachel suddenly exclaimed. "Lookee there, honey," she repeated, delighted at the mysterious surprise. "Them lights just come on."

Lester turned from his wife to the table and saw the glowing bulbs. So it works, he thought. But the thrill he had expected success to bring was absent; Rachel's interruption had botched it. Instead of pleasure, he felt only a sudden wave of fatigue.

Stepping up to the bench, he unscrewed the cap of the jar and unclipped the wires to the battery. Then he turned back to Rachel and took her arm.

"Nothin', honey," he said matter-of-factly. "I ain't doin' nothin'. Just messin' around." He recognized now how absurd his momentary terror had been. It was the way she had come up on him, startling him like that. It had unnerved him. "Let's go up to bed," he coaxed.

Rachel nodded vaguely, acquiescing to his pressure on her arm. At the door, she looked back over her shoulder for a moment, as if making one last effort to understand what was going on. Then Lester flicked the light switch, and the little room went black.

Over the weekend, he resolved as he led Rachel toward the stairs, he would build a mockup of the shelf in the sub-basement, stick the plumbing pipe through it, and cut a hole the size of a brick in the back panel. Then he could practice placing the charge.

20

THE TWO "OUTSIDE EXPERTS" were already seated at the conference table when Calman Richards escorted Hanson into the room. More like an operating theater, Paul reflected. The room's atmosphere, save for the warmth of the burnished wooden table, was cold and sterile, its antiseptic quality emphasized by the harsh fluorescent lighting.

Richards motioned casually in the direction of a chair halfway along one side, then moved away from Paul toward the head of the table—if the rounded end of an oval merited such a designation. As he settled into the suggested seat, Paul took a closer look at the two strangers—and recognized them. The big, florid man with an incongruously dignified and impressive mane of silver-gray hair was Dr. Evan Walter, Chief of the Reactor Safety Division at Argonne National Laboratory. He was sitting with loosely folded arms diagonally across the table to Paul's right. The other man, diagonally across the table on the left, Hanson recognized as Dr. Cleanth Rombart, Chairman of the Department of Nuclear Physics at Stanford University. As a foil to Walter's ruddy, imposing massiveness, Rombart seemed even more pale and frail than Paul recalled. Though he had been briefly introduced to both men at last year's meeting of the American Nuclear Society, he doubted that either remembered him.

Big guns, Paul thought—the biggest. Suddenly he cursed the stupid naiveté that had led him to take the chair Richards had pointed out with such apparently unstudied casualness. In doing so, he had allowed Richards to engineer a subtle antagonism, had helped him to create "sides," and had permitted him to effectively remove himself from the lines of fire across the table. Paul now realized that he, Walter, and Rombart formed an isosceles triangle. The line between Walter and Rombart constituted the base; the two men themselves were the corners. And the lines of both equilateral sides converged directly on Paul at the apex. Richards, at the end of the table, could observe, listen, and comment from outside the triangle; from his clever perch, he could snipe at will with minimum risk of getting caught in the battle proper.

As Paul stumbled through the introductions, he realized that Richards had engineered this awkwardness, too. There were many other men in the field equally expert but less famous than Rombart and Walter, men with whom Hanson would have stood as equal to equal, with whom an introduction would have been two-sided rather than one-sided, and to whom Hanson would not have had to say, "I already know who you are; in fact, we were introduced last year"—men, in short, to whom the introductions would not have been "Mr. Somebody, meet Mr. Nobody." Paul decided that he heartily disliked Mr. Sly Fatman Calman Richards.

What followed did nothing to mitigate his judgment. For no sooner were the introductions completed than he was treated to a further display of Richards's stage management. As if on cue, the doors of the conference room opened, and in trouped a procession of staff people: a stenographer, a couple of bland research types, and a tall, erect man bearing the ineluctable demeanor of an attorney. They arrayed themselves in chairs along the back wall, across the room from Hanson, neither speaking nor spoken to.

"Now, then," Richards said, "let me just briefly review what I've explained to each of you individually, so we can all be sure we're on the same wavelength." Folding hand over fist on the table before him, he summarized the purpose and the ground rules of the meeting.

"So," Richards concluded, "I think the most expeditious procedure would be for you, Dr. Hanson, to first recapitulate for us your reservations about safety considerations at Sand Beach. Then, after you have set forth the matters that concern you, Doctors Walter and Rombart can respond and ask questions."

Paul realized that Richards's presentation had put him at a

further disadvantage. The burden of proof was to be his. The two-member panel of experts would listen, question, and comment. Richards would be the judge. It wasn't to be the formal hearing he had requested, but it *was* an inquiry, and the panelists were well-credentialed and presumptively fairminded. He cleared his throat, leaned forward to rest his forearms on the table, glanced first at Rombart, then at Walter, and began his exposition.

"Mr. Richards informed me that copies of my letter were distributed"—he waited until both men across from him made slight, noncommittal nods—"so I won't repeat all that I wrote there. Instead, I'll simply try to set forth the essential safety issue, as I see it. That issue breaks down into two components, and the crucial issue in each case is credibility."

Glancing quickly at each face around the table, Hanson found no clues, only inscrutable attentiveness. "The first component is the degree to which the Sand Beach reactor is safeguarded by its various scram systems from the possibility of a major power excursion, an excursion of sufficient magnitude to produce substantial core disassembly. If, in the event of a super-prompt-critical power transient, these safety systems are capable of successfully scramming the reactor—if, in short, they possess absolute credibility—then the matter of the second component and its credibility becomes irrelevant, and I would not be here today. But, to me, these systems lack that absolute credibility. They lack credibility because of two unique characteristics of the Sand Beach reactor, one deliberate, one unanticipated.

"Sand Beach is one of the few fast-breeder reactors using the new advanced ceramic fuel. The properties of this new alloy, as you know, allow the fuel pins to function at a much higher operating temperature than was possible with the old material—and thus greatly increase the Plant's operational efficiency. But, as everyone agrees, that increased efficiency has been achieved at the expense of some reduction in the margin of safety."

Paul realized that he was lecturing, and cautioned himself. Nevertheless, the background, even though familiar to all of

108

them, had to be sketched, for only in that context did his fears make sense.

"The trade-off between efficiency and safety was, of course, a conscious and considered choice. It was concluded that a sufficient safety margin would still remain. But the other potentially hazardous characteristic of Sand Beach was not deliberate—its uniquely short reactor period under certain conditions."

Glancing from Walter to Rombart to Richards, he noted that he had regained their full attention. The use of the new ceramic alloy at Sand Beach was common knowledge; the fact that some as yet inexplicable design defect had resulted in a reactor period of less than half that intended was known to only a handful of physicists within the nuclear-power establishment. He was pleased at the advantage his reference to that guarded bit of information gave him. Simultaneously, he realized that his voice had gained both resonance and forcefulness. That was good, for he was now coming to his main point about the scram systems. He allowed the pause to lengthen a while longer in order that it might lend further emphasis to his peroration.

"In my three years as Operations Supervisor at Sand Beach, the reactor has undergone four power surges of such intensity that the reactor-period scram was automatically triggered. In each instance, the automatic scram proved capable of terminating the power surge before that surge could in turn trigger a nuclear runaway. However, the point is that *normal* power transients—that is, power surges recognized as part of the day-to-day operation of any nuclear reactor—surges that should have been compensated for by routine control-rod adjustment—were mitigated only by the *emergency* measure of scramming the reactor.

"If a routine transient leads to the threshold of nuclear runaway and requires *emergency* measures for its control, what would happen in the event of a non-routine reactivity insertion, a rapid insertion of large amounts of reactivity? I submit that such an abnormal reactivity insertion—such as that which would follow loss of core coolant, cladding failure, a refueling accident, or a dozen other possibilities—might well lead to super-prompt-criticality and major core disassembly *before* the scram systems could take effect."

End of Part One, Paul observed to himself. Sitting back in his chair, he felt suddenly fatigued, and realized how much energy he must have expended in making the presentation. But the crucial part still lay ahead. He could not afford to be tired.

Walter and Rombart, like two middle-aged Bobbsey twins, nodded in unison. Richards remained expressionless, revealing no sign of his feelings.

"It's unfortunate," Walter observed to nobody in particular. "That short folding time."

"Plays hell with all the other calculations," Rombart commented.

"Why don't you go ahead and finish," Richards told Hanson.

Paul nodded, ignoring the overtones and undertones in Richards's command. So far, he felt, the Bobbsey twins were both with him. Richards could go to hell. When he continued, he concentrated his gaze on Walter and Rombart.

"For these reasons," Hanson said, "it seems probable that credible accidents, such as those I mentioned, could have consequences at Sand Beach far more serious than if they occurred at any other reactor. Instead of being controlled by automatic scram, without damage to the reactor core, such accidents might well result in a super-prompt-critical power transient followed by gross core disassembly.

"If that should happen, then the motion of molten fuel *might*—and I stress that word, *might*—be capable of creating a recriticality event with major explosive potential. That's a risk we dare not take."

Spreading his hands on the table top, he hunched forward and prepared, like a symphony conductor, to orchestrate a convincing crescendo. "If Sand Beach is vulnerable to accident-triggered gross core disassembly, and I believe it is, I simply do not see how its continued operation can be justified until we have assured ourselves that such disassembly could not possibly produce a nuclear explosion capable of breaching the containment."

Hanson was surprised at how rapidly he had rushed from Part One through Part Two, from convincing premise to hard-to-accept conclusion—and at how abstract and hypothetical it had all sounded. If only he could put the problem in plain English, he thought, tell it straight and simple like it was. Just say, "Look, the reactor is like a boiler. If too much heat is injected into a boiler, without any means to draw it off, it will explode. The same with Sand Beach. If scram fails, the reactor core could overheat and begin to melt. If it melts in such a way that a lot of fuel got compacted quickly, it could explode, just like a steam boiler—but a million times more destructively." That's what it was really all about, when you cut through the jargon. But you weren't allowed to talk about it that way.

He slumped back and, almost disinterestedly, watched the others watch him, in silence, for at least a full minute. He was satisfied with his presentation; he saw no way it could have been better, given the rules one had to follow. Whether it had been sufficiently effective, however, remained to be seen.

When, two hours and a hundred questions later, Richards thanked him and dismissed him, he realized that he had failed. They had accepted, he could tell, his assessment of Sand Beach's liability to core disassembly. What they refused to accept was any possibility that such a power-excursion-induced meltdown might lead to the violent, coherent, and massive fuel motion necessary to trigger a nuclear explosion of sufficient force to breach the secondary containment. That hypothesized eventuality, they had each maintained—Richards and Walter explicitly, Rombart implicitly in a related observation—was simply not credible.

Since there was no known means by which the Sand Beach reactor's transient period could be lengthened, the installation would have to remain in operation. The worst that could happen—and, barring a major accident, it was improbable—was a substantial core meltdown. It was unanimously agreed that such a meltdown would forever destroy the Plant's reactor, yet pose no health hazard to either plant or civilian personnel. That being the case, the closing of the Sand Beach nuclear facility was not justified.

Paul returned home on the seven-o'clock flight from Washington's Dulles Field, knowing he had destroyed his career for nothing. As he drained his second Scotch, he recalled a comment Calman Richards had made toward the end of the meeting; one of the few interjections of personal opinion the NRC chairman had allowed himself.

"You're just crying wolf," Richards had said.

COUNTDOWN

21

"NOW WHAT DO WE DO?" Sherry asked him that night after he had recounted the story of the hearing.

But Paul felt too drained even to contemplate staggering from the sofa to bed, much less fighting for a cause. He had been up before six to catch the eight-thirty A.M. commuter flight to Washington. Then there had been the tension of the interminable three-hour wait before the meeting was scheduled to begin. Then almost three hours in the meeting itself. And finally the whole process of taxi, flight, and driving back, bringing him home at last. And all to no avail. "Nothing," he muttered, slouching down farther on the sofa. "There's nothing more we can do."

Sherry regarded him incredulously. "You mean you'll just go on working until they fire you, and then we'll simply pack up and leave? Say, 'Thanks for the screw job,' stick our tails between our legs, and scuttle off?"

"That's about the size of it," Paul agreed. He felt too dispirited to argue.

"But what about all the people you think are in danger?"

"What about them?" Paul said.

"You can't just leave them!" Sherry cried. "Besides, we're part of them—you and me and Katie. If you don't care about anyone else, at least you care about us."

"We'll be leaving," Paul replied. "The rest can go hang."

That cynical, calloused statement caused Sherry to draw herself away from his side in genuine repugnance. "You can't mean that."

Paul sighed. "No, I don't mean that. I'm just tired." He rattled the ice cubes in his glass. "Make me another drink, and I'll try to explain what we're up against. Then, like it or not, I'm going to bed."

When Sherry returned, he accepted the replenished Scotch and water without looking up.

"I'm no prophet," he said as she settled back on the couch, sitting on her legs, keeping a certain wary, distrustful distance between her body and his. "I'm no genius, either." He worked up enough energy to roll his head, and found her watching him attentively, withholding final judgment. "Probably a hundred different physicists, men just like me, helped in the design of Sand Beach. If any of them, any *one* of them, had found something wrong, something dangerous, he would have said so.

"You don't know the two men at the hearing, Rombart and Walter, but you can take my word. They're both international authorities; there isn't a physicist in the country who doesn't know their names and their work." He raised his hands a few inches, then let them fall back to his lap in expressive resignation. "All these people say I'm wrong. None of them sees even the slightest possibility that Sand Beach could explode in such a way that the dome integrity would be compromised."

He rolled his head again, met Sherry's eyes, and saw that he had regained her trust. Her eyes were misting in sympathy. "So who am I," he continued, "to go against the weight of such authority? I got carried away, that's all. It happens all the time in the field. A guy conceives a theory, shouts around about it, and in the process grows so enamored of it that he won't let it go when the evidence refuting his pet idea piles up. So, he ends up making an ass of himself, and loses his credibility—just like me."

"But you're *right!*" Sherry exclaimed, now enthusiastically on his side again. "Those people you're talking about were wrong. But you're right!"

"Maybe," Paul said. He lifted the glass to his lips and drained it. "I'm going to bed now."

22

LESTER SAT ON THE TOILET in the Administration Building's executive washroom, his pants and undershorts dropped about his ankles for the sake of appearance. For the first time in more years than he cared to remember, he actually laughed. It had gone off without a hitch.

The pre-shaped diamond charge was strapped against his back. The lunch pail on the floor by his feet contained the transistor radio with its essential battery, the jar of dried peas (the three inconspicuous holes in its lid had not even been noticed), two screws, and a half-pint jar of water. Taped to the back of his oversized belt buckle, cozy in their tightly coiled wire nests, were the two blasting caps, backed by the small tin disk which would complete the firing circuit.

That had been one of his triumphs—figuring out a way to smuggle the blasting caps and tin disk past the airport-type metal scanner through which all employees entering the Plant were required to pass. He had found the solution in a store that specialized in Western garb: buckskin jackets, chaps, ten-gallon Stetson hats, string ties, hand-crafted boots, ornate jewelry—all the crap one needed to make himself into a perfect ass.

"That's a beautiful buckle, sir," the duded-up clerk simpered as Lester hefted the silver-plated monstrosity. "Our most popular."

Lester pulled a retractable tape measure from his coat pocket and, as the clerk watched in puzzlement, determined the buckle's dimensions. Fully three inches by four, he noted—plenty big enough. The damned thing must weigh half a pound.

"How much?" he asked, returning the tape measure to his pocket.

"It's silver-plated," the clerk responded. "And notice the carving, all done by hand."

By hand my ass, Lester thought. These things were stamped out by the thousand. "How much?" he repeated.

"Forty-five dollars, sir. And worth every penny," the clerk hastened to add.

"Too much," Lester stated with finality, dropping it on the counter. The buckle clanged against the glass counter top with the force of an angle iron, evoking a gasp of horror from the clerk.

"Glass is stronger than you think," Lester said. He had begun to enjoy himself: the only man in a storeful of faggots.

"Do you have something like it, but cheaper? Maybe in plastic?"

The clerk was obviously reluctant to lose his commission on the high-priced buckle, but a glance at Cuthright's features convinced him it was hopeless. "Well," he drawled, affecting a falsetto twang, "as a matter of fact, we do have an inexpensive version of the same buckle." His disapproval of anything inexpensive came through, and Lester noticed that he had dropped the "sir." "It is, as I said, our most popular design. And some do find the real thing a bit dear." His tone left no doubt as to his view of such people.

"Let's see it," Lester said.

"This way," the clerk said.

"Bring it here," Lester said. He wanted to make a comparison.

When the clerk returned, he no longer pretended politeness. He flicked the plastic buckle onto the counter top without comment.

Lester ignored him, studying the quality of the imitation. It wasn't bad. Whatever was painted on the surface of the plastic buckle would probably begin to wear off after a few weeks of handling, but until that happened, the plastic and the metal buckles were indistinguishable except for the fake's slightly glossier sheen.

"I'll take both," Lester said, shoving the pair across the counter toward the clerk.

118

When he wore the metal buckle the very next day, the metal scanner had screamed in protest. Nolan Kline, Dirk's trained ass-kisser, stopped him the moment he stepped out on the far side of the miniature tunnel.

"I'll have to ask you to empty your pockets, Lester," Kline said. (Lester grinned at the memory. The fact that Kline had been right there this morning, had even given the signal to let him pass when he walked through with the blasting caps—that was sweet.)

He had shrugged, emptied his pockets, and, at Kline's gesture, passed through the tunnel again. Again the machine protested.

"What are you carrying, Lester?" Kline demanded. Lester could tell that the man was truly suspicious now.

"Ain't carrying nothin,'" Lester said, acting surly.

By this time, they had collected a crowd. Something was up. Three other security officers had drifted in from their regular positions at the gate and in the guardhouse.

Kline frisked him but found nothing. Puzzled, he stood back and looked Cuthright up and down. His eyes lit on the buckle.

"What the hell's that?" Kline exclaimed, pointing at the offending slab of metal.

"My belt buckle," Lester said. He could tell that Kline knew he had been made a fool of. Serves the bastard right, Lester thought, remembering the many times Kline had ordered him finger-fucked before he finally got the injunction.

"Take it off," Kline ordered.

"The buckle?"

"No, goddammit! The belt!"

Lester complied, and Kline examined the buckle, turning it over in his hands. Finally, grudgingly, he thrust the belt at Cuthright, muttered disgustedly, and motioned him through.

Every day since then, for almost a month, he had worn the same belt, the same buckle; each time it had triggered the metal scan. Twice in the first week, Kline had strode up and fingered the buckle. After that, he hadn't bothered. The buckle tripped the alarm, Kline glanced at his waist, nodded, the alarm was reset, and Cuthright was motioned on. When he finally substituted the plastic buckle, the metal now being the taped-fast blasting caps and disk, the routine went along just the same.

Like taking candy from a baby, Lester thought to himself as he stripped off his jacket, corduroy shirt, and T-shirt to get at the tape that held the plastic explosive to his back. He had elected to assemble the charge in one of the executive washrooms because, unlike the flunky toilets, where you were under constant surveillance, the executive restrooms were free of monitors. The grapevine said that bigwigs hadn't liked the idea of some punk over in Security watching them on the toilet, and so the overhead monitor had come out. Its bracket and the taped end of its wires made a scar on the room's white ceiling.

Lester piled the clothes on the porcelain pipe behind the toilet bowl, then stripped the tape from his chest. He was far too engrossed to feel pain as hairs came off with the tape. His plan was to preassemble the charge here in the restroom, then transport it to the Diesel Generating Building in his lunch pail at noon. That way, the actual installation would be clean and quick, requiring only three steps. He had them memorized in sequence from relentless practice, and knew the exact time each one required.

23

CLATON, PAUL REFLECTED, had obviously chosen the high
road: martyrdom rather than rage. The man was trying to guilt
him to death.

"I just don't understand how you could have done it, Paul."
Claton sighed. It was at least the tenth sigh, and the fourth or
fifth repetition of the same tired line, since Hanson had
entered the Plant Manager's office to endure this command
performance.

Hanson shifted in his chair, a luxurious, body-contoured,
richly textured armchair, scientifically designed to pleasure
angular human limbs. It wasn't the chair which was causing his
discomfort: he simply didn't know how to respond to Claton's
morose self-pity.

"It's got nothing to do with my feelings toward you," Paul
stated truthfully. "I don't see it that way at all. It's not a
personal thing."

"But it *is* a personal thing," Claton lamented. "Don't you
understand what this is going to do to my career?"

Paul felt his sympathy evaporating. The cat was out of the
bag at last. It wasn't fatherly compassion for a wayward son that
burdened Claton's heart; it was job threat. The chair suddenly
felt more comfortable.

"That's not my fault," Hanson said. "I haven't said anything
against you. Your name has never even come up. It's the
reactor's safety I'm questioning."

"If you doubt that," Claton stated pompously, "you also
cast aspersions on me."

Hanson found this line of reasoning totally absurd. "That's
bullshit," he exclaimed. "There's no connection at all."

"Tell that to Stafford," Claton said. His voice had har-
dened.

"Then Stafford's an ass," Hanson blurted out. "I'm not
responsible for his stupidities."

"That's right," Claton agreed, "you're not." For the first time since Paul had entered the office, Claton's voice rang true, all pretense abandoned. He straightened up in the chair behind his desk, regarding Hanson with cold dislike. "You're not responsible for Stafford's stupidity. You're just responsible for your own."

"The reactor's transient period is less than a millisecond," Hanson stated. "That's too short."

Claton was glaring at him now, his pent-up rage rapidly boiling to the surface. "To hell with your transient period," Claton snorted. "Who do you think you are, anyway?"

When Hanson didn't respond, Claton continued without his cue. "Do you know how many nuclear physicists worked on the design for this goddamned plant?"

"No."

"Hundreds!" Claton exclaimed triumphantly. "And at least a dozen of those were NRC men—Inspectors."

Hanson's only response was an unimpressed shrug. "So?" he said.

"So?" Claton demanded increduously. "So?" He stared at Hanson as though finally convinced that he was speaking to a madman. "So, Sand Beach has so many fail-safe systems you couldn't blow it up with a bomb. And you're yelling and screaming about how it's going to blow up all by itself. Besides, even if it experienced a core-disruptive accident and you were sitting on the reactor vessel, it wouldn't so much as bruise your butt."

"Not blow up exactly," Hanson corrected mildly. "I used the term metaphorically—"

"Metaphorically?" Claton bellowed incredulously. His face was livid. "You want to make metaphors, go be a poet. But not here. Here you're supposed to be a scientist."

"I believe the reactor is susceptible to a meltdown," Hanson stated. As Claton spiraled out of control, he had become increasingly calm. "A major meltdown might produce autocatalytic fuel configurations. If that should happen, it is conceivable that a crude nuclear explosion capable of breaching the containment could be generated."

"Get out of here!" Claton cried. He leaped to his feet with such force that his chair slammed against the wall.

"You're finished," he added as Hanson rose. "There's not a company in the country that'll hire you after what you've done here."

"I'm quite aware of that," Hanson said, meeting Claton's reddened eyes. Then the banal absurdity of the confrontation washed over him, killing the flow of adrenalin. He turned and walked out of the office.

24

IN THE BASEMENT of the Diesel Generator Building, Lester slouched on the brick shelf in his accustomed position, chewing but not tasting his sandwich, lunch pail open as usual beside him. Covertly he studied the slow-swinging camera that automatically monitored the room. The camera operated on a three-minute scan, moving from the far left to the far right and back in that time. Lester knew because he had timed it. There were, however, two uncertainties. Even though he was sitting near the extreme end of the camera's far-right sweep, he wasn't sure exactly how close. He figured he had to allow thirty seconds from the time it began to sweep left in order to be certain it had passed him, and another thirty seconds on its way back. That gave him a safe working time of a hundred twenty seconds. The other uncertainty stemmed from the fact that all the monitors were subject to instant manual override by personnel in Security Control. Since he could do nothing about that fact, he had decided to ignore it. Long since, he had resolved that if he rose from behind the shelf and found the camera locked in on him, he would detonate the charge and go with it.

On the cement floor behind the shelf on which he sat, everything lay in readiness. Now he removed one final piece of equipment from the lunch pail: a miniature hourglass egg timer. At home, he had prised off one end and emptied enough sand so that, instead of three minutes, exactly two were required for it all to flow from the top of the hourglass to the bottom. When the hourglass touched the surface of the brickwork behind the lunch pail, which would shield it from the camera's eye, Lester felt it skitter. His hand was trembling.

Deliberately, despite his distaste, he took another bite out of the sandwich. As he chewed, the food gritty in his dry mouth, he tried to force calm by mentally reciting the practice-familiar stages in installing the charge. Stage One, he repeated to himself: pull brick, position battery, place charge, tape charge—thirty-five seconds. Stage Two: strip insulating safety tape from poles on lid, pour water into jar, insert tin disk, tighten lid—forty-five seconds. Stage Three: tape trip line to inner side of brick, reinsert brick—twenty seconds. Total— one hundred seconds. Safety margin—twenty seconds. Nothing to it. Saliva oozed into his mouth, and he swallowed the wad of food. It was time to get started.

When the television monitor reached its full-right position and then started its slow arc back to his left, Lester began a silent countdown, starting with thirty. When he reached "one," he glanced at the camera, saw that it was continuing its swing, flipped the hourglass upside down, swung his legs up, pivoted on his haunches, and crouched behind the shelf.

The brick came free without sticking. Setting it to one side, he inserted the battery and the uncapped, pea-filled olive jar first, lowering them until they touched the floor of the cavity. Then he shoved the battery to the right, out of the way. Withdrawing his hand, he fumbled for the plastic explosive, and slipped the tightly rolled charge through the hole, careful to keep a firm grip on the tip of its uppermost longitudinal axis, which was the key to unrolling the charge. His left hand followed his right and assisted in unrolling the plastic croissant. That accomplished, the left hand withdrew, and Lester, able to reach farther, maneuvered the charge up and over the electrical conduit. In the momentary relief that successful action evoked, Lester had a quick flash of the strange sight he must make, wedged behind the shelf in a strained frog-legged squat, his chin almost touching the shelf's surface, eyes popping with his effort.

The vision died as he groped for the dangling piece of tape with which to mate the two ends of the charge. He felt it brush against his fingers, then lost it. He groped again, found it, and pinched too hard, sealing it against his finger.

Despite the press of time, he disengaged the tape slowly, taking infinite care; a hasty motion might jerk the far end off

125

the charge. When his finger was finally free of the sticky embrace, he brought the tape up, found the loose end of the charge, and secured it tight against the other.

End of Stage One, Lester told himself. But he suspected he had used up most of his safety margin. As he reached for the water jar, he glanced at the hourglass. Its different shapes—tight funnel on top, flat bottom below—made it impossible to read the sand. He didn't bother to look up toward the camera. At this point, it was no longer a factor.

Uncapping the jar of water with the palm of his right hand, he got a good grip and worked it through the hole in the shelf, rasping his knuckles in the process. The diameter of the jar, squat and wide to fit through the shallow opening, caused his thumb to stick out straight. As he probed blindly and too quickly for the olive jar, he stabbed a needle-sharp outcropping of mortar deep beneath his thumbnail. The uncontrollable spasm triggered by that searing penetration broke his grip on the water jar. He knew, even before it hit, that it would break. It did. The sound of shattered glass, though muted by the brick shield, was impossible to mistake.

Lester felt himself beginning to panic. Convinced that he had been discovered, he craned his neck to spot the camera. It was just beginning its return swing back to the right. He still had forty, maybe fifty, seconds.

That realization—the knowledge that he was undiscovered and had time remaining—calmed him. Just go ahead and do the rest, he told himself; the water can be added any time. The unspoken advice came as a revelation. In his preoccupation with getting the job done in one swift sequence, he had somehow failed to understand that it could just as well be spaced out over a whole series of lunch hours, especially since he had added the extra precaution of the trip line.

Retrieving the tin disk and safety-taped jar lid from the floor, he pulled cautiously on the disk until he had a couple of feet of slack in the heavy nylon thread that ran from the disk through a hole in the center of the lid. Then, groping with utmost caution, he found the olive jar. With the disk in position, he stripped the electrician's tape from the two poles in the lid and ran the lid down the nylon trip line until it positioned itself atop the jar.

Leaving the lid loose—there was no point in tightening it until the water was added—he painstakingly took the slack out of the thread, going by sight as well as feel. A slip-up here would kill him.

When the thread looked and felt just barely taut, he brought up the brick with his left hand, gave himself two inches of slack, and taped the trip line securely to the brick's inner face. Then, the booby trap set, he pushed the brick back into place. Straightening, he glanced at the hourglass. The last grains of sand fell even as he watched.

A few seconds later, seated on the shelf, the sandwich again in his hand, Lester's peripheral vision observed the camera swing lazily by. Suddenly, for the second time on this red-letter day, he felt an urge to laugh. Three minutes before a malignant enemy, the camera was now a mere joke. Like an adult recalling an absurd childhood dream, Lester could scarcely believe he had feared it. He felt very good.

The idea must have been germinating deep in his unconscious, for it suddenly burst on him in full, glorious bloom. He would wait a few days before adding the water—maybe even a week or two—enjoy for a while this new feeling of power and mastery. After all, the charge was rigged to explode if anyone pulled out the brick—pulled it out, that is, without knowing what he was doing. That was the beauty of the trip line—and why he had had to be so careful attaching it. Of course, when the idea for the fail-safe device had first occurred to him, he had been thinking in quite different terms.

The device was a nighttime creation, the offspring of a waking nightmare in which the charge—emplaced, rigged, and watered—somehow was discovered before the slowly expanding peas could force the tin disk up against the two lid screws. Even at that time, he had recognized the absurd paranoia implied in the scenario, yet—still—it was possible. And with his fingerprints on everything . . .

Hence the trip line. He had drilled a tiny hole in the center of the tin disk, run an extra-strong nylon thread through it, and knotted the end. When he had taped that thread to the inner face of the brick, he had left two inches of slack, just enough to allow him to detach the taped thread without disturbing the tin plate. It was inconceivable that anyone else discovering that de-mortared brick would be so cautious. The impulse would be to give it a healthy tug and pull it free, to peer into the cavity beyond. But instead of a look, they would get his surprise. The thread would pull the disk, the disk would touch the screws, and the firing circuit would be completed.

So why not? Lester thought. He risked nothing. After the new feeling wore off, that would be the time to add the water.

When the camera next swung away from him, Lester retrieved the lid of the broken jar, deposited the hourglass in his lunch pail, and, whistling under his breath, headed for the elevator. He was totally unaware of the throbbing purple lake beneath his thumbnail.

25

JUST FROM SHERRY'S TONE OF VOICE, Paul could tell she was excited and impressed. Cupping her hand over the phone's mouthpiece, eyes sparkling, she announced, sotto voce, "It's long distance—Washington. They're calling for John Henderson!"

Even as he pushed his chair away from the dinner table, Hanson considered and rejected the likelihood that the caller was a crank. It had been inevitable.

"John Henderson!" Sherry reiterated in a dramatic stage whisper as Paul rose and moved toward her.

The only acknowledgment he could manage was an unenthusiastic nod. It was all going to be taken out of his hands now; it was going to get out of control. And even though he had half suspected from the very beginning that this might be the eventual upshot, he did not welcome the confirmation. From now on, it would become messy and, almost certainly, nasty as well. As the one who started it, he would have no choice but to see it through. He took the receiver from Sherry's eager hands with fatalistic resignation.

"Yes?"

"Dr. Paul Hanson?" The voice was female.

"Yes."

"One moment, sir, for John Henderson." Paul waited. The moment stretched to a minute, then two. Finally, he heard the clicks that signified a new connection.

"Dr. Hanson, this is John Henderson in Washington. Of course, I don't expect you to simply accept my word for that, so may I ask—"

"I believe you," Hanson stated, interrupting.

"Well," Henderson said, after a momentary, nonplussed pause. "Then you must know why I'm calling."

"Yes," Hanson said.

"We're going to run the story on Sand Beach the day after

tomorrow," Henderson said. "We have a copy of Cal Richards's memo regarding your meeting with him. But we would like to flesh it out, set forth the whole issue rather than just expose the charade of that so-called inquiry he engineered to shut you up. In order to do that, we need an interview. One of my staff can be at your house at seven o'clock tomorrow morning, if you're willing to talk with him." Henderson let a pause develop, then added, "It will all come out eventually, no matter what you do."

Hanson did not take umbrage at Henderson's smug clincher. His comment was not a boast, merely a fact. Once the story made the news, nothing could be hidden. It was simply a question of whether he spoke now or later. "I'll talk with him," Hanson said.

"But I don't want to be famous," Paul protested with absolute sincerity later that evening. The imminent likelihood of becoming a *cause célèbre* was totally repugnant.

Sherry smiled at his disclaimer with indulgent skepticism. "Everyone wants to be famous," she asserted.

"Even when it's going to cost them their job?"

Sherry's smile broadened to a grin. "You can always teach." She laughed. "Universities love people who fall in the battle for a noble cause. At least," she amended, "that's what my father always said, and he should know."

Indeed he should, Paul acknowledged. For fully fifteen years, right up until his sudden coronary and death four summers ago, Sherry's father had been a popular and respected professor of social economics. The sole basis for his reputation, and hence his successful university career, was the fact that, at age forty-two, having enjoyed a meteoric rise to the highest ranks of automobile magnates, he had suddenly done an about-face and publicly denounced the private gasoline-powered passenger car as the country's greatest scourge. He trumpeted that virtually every evil that plagued the nation, every rent in the social fabric, every social, economic, and environmental malaise from which the country suffered, emanated directly or indirectly from America's suicidal love affair with the private

130

automobile. The petroleum imports necessary to sustain these monstrous wheeled vermin impoverished the country, converting a potential balance-of-trade surplus into a staggering deficit. The construction and maintenance of the concrete blankets on which these creatures scurried about drained the treasury while simultaneously scarring the land. The mobility they provided was responsible not only for urban sprawl but for the death throes of the major cities as well, each vehicle bringing into a city's heart its poisonous gases, traffic jams as life-choking as blood clots in an artery, clamor, and the destructive hostility of maddened drivers; each vehicle, each evening, fleeing with a day's blood money to suburbia, there to spill it, such libations providing perilous life to bedroom communities while killing the urban heart on which they ultimately depended.

And so it went, on and on. Students loved it. No lecture series was complete without him. The university that had taken him in congratulated itself, promoted him, and basked in the fame of his name. But, of course, his fifteen years of proselytizing had had no significant effect whatsoever on the loathsome love affair he had daily excoriated.

No, Paul reflected, such fruitless theatrics were not his cup of tea. He had grown fond of his father-in-law, had respected his unflagging energy and zeal, had even finally been persuaded to his thesis. But the thought of long labor in the service of a hopeless cause left him cold. He would grant the interview because he believed his fears were valid and felt conscience-bound to affirm them. He would speak out in any respectable public forum that the publicity generated by Henderson's exposé might create. Then, having had his say, he would seek a position in a quiet, research-oriented university and leave the shouting to others. The thought of whether or not he might enjoy staying on at Sand Beach never entered his mind. The inevitable letter of termination was already overdue.

26

THE FEW DAYS OF FEELING GOOD Lester had allotted himself before watering the peas, as he liked to think of it, had stretched to almost three weeks, and yet he had made no move to prime the timer. In fact, the longer he delayed, the less urgent it all seemed.

For five years, ever since Eric's birth, he had been like the puny schoolboy everybody bullied. Feeling victimized, yet powerless to strike back, he had been obsessed by fantasies of retribution. Planting the charge had transformed him: through that single act, he had wrested the reins of fate from the hands of others, and made them his own.

He had not abandoned his resolve to eventually detonate the explosive, but it had become somehow less important, whether he didn't or did. What was important was the knowledge that he could, if he so chose, that he had the power, that the decision was his alone.

Two disturbing thoughts had occurred to Lester during this interval. One was that—just possibly—the radiation exposure he had received at the Green Valley plant might not be the sole cause of Eric's deformity. The other was an intuition that, through his withdrawal and sullen anger, he himself might have contributed to Rachel's alcoholism. He had rejected both ideas, suppressing them almost instantly. But it was a measure of the radical change in him that such notions had been even briefly allowed to penetrate his consciousness.

It was as though he were wearing a new pair of eyeglasses which altered his perception of a long-familiar and accepted reality, revealing multiple shadings where before he had seen only light and shadow. For the first time in three years, he had made real love to Rachel, tenderly, as to a person hurt, trying as best she could to cope. Having planted the bomb, he had regained the capacity to feel compassion.

132

27

THE STAFFER FROM Henderson's Washington office was young, clean-cut, sincere, and almost fanatically intense: unmistakably a youthful crusader with a passionate zeal for Good.

Hanson had risen at six A.M., an hour earlier than usual, in order to be fully awake by the time the man arrived. Having showered, shaved, and dressed, he was seated at the breakfast table sipping his third cup of black coffee when he heard tires crunching on the drive. Glancing at his watch, he noted that it was precisely seven o'clock.

"Dr. Hanson?" the man said. His eagerly extended hand was thrust out even before Hanson had fully opened the door.

"Paul," Hanson said, accepting the proffered handshake. The man's grip was firm, but not aggressively so; his palm was dry, neither hot nor cold; his clear blue eyes met Hanson's noncommittal gray ones with friendly candor. He was as wholesome as a Norman Rockwell apple pie.

Jesus, Hanson thought, how could one resist? He decided not to bother trying. Returning the man's smile, he stepped back to let him enter.

"My name's Chris Kendall," the young man announced. He extracted an envelope from the inside pocket of his sports jacket and offered it to Hanson. "John Henderson gave me this to identify myself."

Hanson nodded, accepted the envelope, and used it as a pointer to indicate the kitchen table. Sherry and Katie were still asleep. When Katie woke up, they would have to move to his study. In the meantime, though, the kitchen seemed less formal, brighter, and more inviting. "Can I get you a cup of coffee?"

"Great!" Chris exclaimed. "I finished off the thermos in the car an hour ago."

Although Kendall had probably spent most of last night preparing for this meeting, and the rest of it driving, he showed no signs of fatigue. Youth, Paul reflected wryly. Kendall couldn't be more than six or seven years his junior, but those were a few years that made a big difference. "Black or white?" he asked.

"Black."

Hanson set the mug on the table top and motioned Kendall an invitation to sit down. After topping off his own cup, Paul took a seat across from him, tapped the end of the envelope on the table, and tore off a narrow strip. After a brief glance at the letterhead, which bore Henderson's name in discrete block capitals and the title of his organization, Hanson turned his attention to the text. The letter was brief and succinct.

"This will introduce Chris Kendall," he read. "Chris has worked on matters involving nuclear-generated power on earlier occasions and is knowledgeable, though by no means an expert, in this area. He has also informed himself, insofar as the time available permitted, concerning the construction, operating history, and special characteristics of the Sand Beach Nuclear Power Generating Facility. I appreciate your willingness to talk with him."

The letter was signed "Cordially," a fact that Paul Hanson found strangely agreeable—it was his own preferred closing.

Setting the letter to one side, he glanced up and found Kendall watching him expectantly.

"Would you object to my using a tape recorder?" Kendall inquired. As he spoke, he moved to unsling a black vinyl case at his side, suspended by a strap slung over his shoulder. Hanson was surprised he hadn't noticed the apparatus earlier.

"I'd rather you didn't," he said without reflection. The unrehearsed objection came as an additional surprise, for he had nothing to hide.

"Notes, then?" Kendall asked agreeably, lowering the recorder to the floor.

"Notes are fine," Hanson said. He was used to dictation.

134

The deftness with which Kendall extracted a stenographer's pad from his coat pocket, flipped it open, and made a pen appear in his fingers told Hanson the man took expert shorthand. He realized he was going to be recorded anyway.

"What we're primarily interested in is your view of the safety hazards," Kendall observed. "What incidents motivated you to write the NRC, what you feel are the dangers posed by Sand Beach, that sort of thing."

Hanson nodded his understanding. "I don't know whether you've run a background check on me or not."

Kendall made no sign that would either confirm or deny this suspicion.

"If you have," Hanson continued after a moment, "you know that my specialty is fast-reactor safety."

Kendall nodded in encouragement, giving no indication as to whether the information was old or new. Silence descended. After a few moments, Hanson recognized the ploy, but did not find it objectionable. Some ten years before, while still a graduate student, before he had met Sherry, he had paid several visits to a psychiatrist. The problem had been minor and transitory, and had never disturbed him since. He doubted that the psychiatrist had contributed one way or another to its solution. But those visits remained vivid in his memory, not because of what he had or had not confessed, but because they had been his first, and most dramatic, introduction to the compelling power of silent listening. In those several hour-long sessions, the psychiatrist had spoken no more than a few dozen words. His intense, expectant, disciplined silence had had the effect of forcing Paul to talk. And, before each hour was out, that silence had made him talk more honestly than he had ever talked before.

Such was the familiar technique Kendall was employing. And since Hanson had bottled up things he wished to say, both then, on the psychiatrist's couch, and now, at his kitchen table, the ploy was effective.

"I think that the ultimate integrity of the Sand Beach

containment is doubtful," Hanson said. "In the event of a major meltdown, it might be breached. That's the whole thing in a nutshell."

From Kendall there was a faint nod of encouragement—and continued silence.

Hanson took a sip of coffee. Then, settling to a more comfortable position in his chair, he began to elaborate.

28

EARL STAFFORD HAD A HELICOPTER READY on the roof and one of the Company's Lear jets standing by at Kennedy airport, for he intended to wring out that extra bit of gratitude that would come with delivering glad tidings personally. Thanks to his preparations, he was ushered into Cal Richards's Washington office less than two hours after the Board meeting in New York adjourned. When Richards's first words were a complaint, Stafford knew his scheme to be first with the news had succeeded.

"I hear you still have that bastard physicist up at Sand Beach," Richards said.

Stafford took a seat without invitation. You knew you were on Richards's good side when he reverted to his natural rudeness. It was when he started oozing etiquette that you had to watch out.

"We're working on it, Cal," Stafford told him. "Can't just go out and grab somebody off the street, you know. But we've got some good prospects. Should be able to get him out in a couple of weeks, three at the most."

Richards glowered, unplacated. "The sooner the better." Hunching forward in his chair, he planted his stubby forearms on the desk top. "That son of a bitch came this close"—he held up spread thumb and forefingers—"to convincing Rombart and Walter. I wouldn't have believed it if I hadn't seen it myself. He actually had them going. Rombart and Walter," he repeated incredulously.

That fact was news to Stafford. In his letter about the meeting, Richards had simply noted that the prescribed inquiry had been held and Hanson's allegations found to be unsubstantiated. But then, the letter was for the record. "You don't actually suppose . . ." he began.

"Christ, no," Richards interrupted. "He just had 'em going, that's all."

Stafford relaxed, faintly surprised that the thought had even entered his mind. It was that damned e-folding time—it made you wonder if the reactor had other surprises in store.

Stafford thought of his own surprise. Better bring it out before Richards's phone rang. "We had a Board meeting this morning," he said. As he spoke, he raised his attaché case to his lap and freed the latch. "Wanted you to know first thing."

Richards watched quizzically as Stafford rose, set the opened case on the chair, and stepped toward his desk, holding a sheet of paper. The effort at ceremony was a bit awkward, but Stafford did his best to pull it off. Drawing himself erect, he faced Richards across the width of the desk, smiled broadly, and then lowered his eyes to the document in his hand.

" 'By unanimous vote,' " he read aloud, " 'the Board of Directors of Consolidated Power Company, Incorporated, hereby appoints Calman E. Richards, Esquire, to the governing Directorate of the Company, said appointment to become effective upon the date of Mr. Richards's retirement or resignation from the position of Chairman, United States Nuclear Regulatory Commission, subject only to Mr. Richards's acceptance of said position. This appointment is made in recognition and appreciation of Mr. Richards's many contributions to the development and utilization of nuclear-generated power.'

"There's more." Stafford grinned. "All about how great you are." He was gratified to see that Richards looked appropriately taken aback, and pleased.

"There's also quite a handsome honorarium, of course. It's spelled out in the by-laws. I'll send you a copy." Stafford slid through that quickly. Though it was the whole point, custom dictated that it be deemphasized.

"The business at Sand Beach came up," Stafford continued, moving on smoothly, the rough spot now behind him, "and the expert way you handled it. The Board feels that the Company needs such expertise. But mainly"—he smiled, concluding with the requisite piece of banter—"we want to be sure you'll be on our team when you leave the Commission, and not the competition's." Both men laughed together.

138

29

NUCLEAR PHYSICIST PREDICTS
CATASTROPHIC EXPLOSION

Bearing that banner headline, John Henderson's syndicated column appeared in the morning edition of over a hundred newspapers across the country. Henderson had called Paul Hanson Thursday evening to alert him, and warned that the next day would be rough. Nevertheless, Paul was totally unprepared for what ensued.

The first call awakened him at six thirty Friday morning, and turned out to be a crank. With grotesque aptness, it set the tone for a day equally insane.

His main mistake was going to work. Probably no more than a few dozen of the two hundred-odd Sand Beach employees had read Henderson's column before leaving for the Plant that morning, but the grapevine quickly informed, and misinformed, the rest. By the time Paul arrived, at nine thirty, he was a leper.

At the gate, for the first time in all the years of his employment, he was subjected to a search. It wasn't just a *pro forma* inspection of his briefcase, but a harsh body frisk—a procedure normally used to intimidate hourly workers suspected of petty pilfering. Whether the guard was acting on instructions or simply venting his own anger, Paul had no idea. But, whatever its cause, the search made him feel demeaned, and angry.

The walk through the corridors and work areas of the Administration Building convinced Paul that the guard had probably acted on his own, for he met palpable hostility literally at every turn. Gone were the customary smiles, greetings, and friendly nods. In their stead were stares, deliberately turned backs, and silence. He was being frozen out. By the time he finally reached his office, he was sweating.

Sally, his secretary, regarded him with the reproachful

eyes of a devoted and trusting pet betrayed by its master. Even though the telephone on her desk was ringing insistently, the buttons for both outside lines blinking, and all three "hold" buttons glowing, she appeared listless and indifferent.

"Calls were already coming in when I got here," she told him. "A lot of them haven't been very nice."

Paul repressed an impulse to step around her desk and take her in his arms; professional relationships simply didn't allow such personal gestures. Yet that was really what the moment demanded. She had worked happily for him for almost four years, and now, without warning or preamble, he had destroyed his career, thereby putting her own position in jeopardy, and subjected her to obscenity-shouting crazies, too, if the pre-dawn call he had received was any indication.

"I'm sorry," he said. It seemed a lame excuse, incomprehensible even to him. Was he apologizing for the trouble he was causing, or for having turned traitor, or merely for having involved her in it? He wasn't sure.

Still, the apology seemed to help, for Sally managed a smile. It was wan and tentative, but nonetheless a smile, and it warmed the atmosphere in the anteroom considerably.

She held out a sheet of paper. "I've made a list of the important calls." As she spoke, Paul detected a new note in her voice. Whatever her sense of betrayal, her job-threat fear, she sounded impressed. Scanning the list, so was he. The names were all familiar: media personalities representing each of the three major television networks, and nationally known radio and newspaper commentators as well.

"Look," he said, returning his eyes to Sally. "It's just going to get worse. Why don't you take the rest of the day off."

"Are you sure?" she asked. "If this keeps up, you'll need someone to run interference."

"I'm leaving too," Paul said. The announcement came without conscious reflection, as much a surprise to him as to her. "Give me ten minutes to get away, then ring Claton and tell him I got sick and had to go home. As soon as that's done, consider your day over."

Sally nodded but did not meet his eyes. "I'll call Mr.

Claton," she said. "But I think I'd better stay. There really should be someone here to answer the phone, take any messages . . ." Her voice trailed off, the pretense too lame to sustain.

Paul understood. There was no jeopardy in his walking out: he was through anyway. But her case was not so clear-cut. If she played her cards right, remaining efficient and conscientious through the storm, she might avoid falling with him, might manage to stay on, perhaps work for his successor. It was a matter of simple self-preservation.

"Right," he said with forced heartiness. Now they were both avoiding each other's eyes, playing the game through. "I hadn't thought of it that way."

"Shall I indicate you will be back on Monday?"

"Yes, Monday," Paul said. "Maybe things will have settled down by then." He watched as she made a show of noting that fact on a memo pad. Despite the insistent noise of the telephone, the room seemed thick with silence. It was a curious way to say good-bye, since neither of them knew how many days or weeks might pass before it became official.

He stepped to the door, then, awkwardly, turned back. "Well . . . good-bye."

Sally stood. Across the six or seven feet that separated them, Paul could see her face working. "Good-bye, sir," she said.

30

AT ROUGHLY THE SAME TIME Friday morning that Paul Hanson was awakened by the crank call, Lester Cuthright collected the morning newspaper from his stoop, carried it, still folded, to the kitchen, and then began to prepare his customary breakfast of buttered toast, milk, and coffee. Five minutes later, he sat down at the kitchen table, the food before him, and gave a sigh of contentment—Eric and Rachel were both still asleep. With his left hand, he lifted a slice of toast; simultaneously, with his right, he flipped open the newspaper. The toast never reached his mouth. With Sand Beach the largest employer in the newspaper's circulation area, the editors had elected to headline Henderson's column on page one.

After reading the first few lines of the story, Cuthright paused, pushed away food and drink, and repositioned the newspaper directly in front of him. Then he read through the account three times in succession.

Had he been asked, before reading Hanson's allegation, whether the Sand Beach reactor could possibly, under any circumstances, explode, he would have responded with an unequivocal "No." Yet never for an instant did he doubt Hanson's charges. There were two reasons for his absolute and instantaneous certainty that Hanson spoke the truth. One was that he liked the man. Unlike most of the managerial staff, who either ignored him or clearly despised him, Hanson always greeted him pleasantly, by name, whenever they passed each other in a room or corridor. But the main reason he accepted Hanson's allegations implicitly was that in order for Hanson's charges to be true, the Company had to have been lying. And Lester *knew* the Company lied.

The Company had pretended to believe that the radiation dosage he had received had not caused Eric's deformity; in pretending that, they had lied. The Company had maintained, propagandized, and assured that the Sand Beach reactor could not, under any conditions, explode; Hanson said it could. So, once again, unquestionably, the Company was lying.

The monstrous villainy of that lie enraged him. It was a lie that, had Hanson not exposed it when he did, would have resulted in his exposing thousands, maybe tens of thousands, of innocent persons to the same sort of radiation that had made a horror of his son. The thought of that consequence of his intended revenge sickened him. Lurching out of the kitchen toward the bathroom, he grasped the toilet seat and dry-heaved white mucus into the bowl.

When he finally rose, purged, he looked hopefully at his watch. But time had not stood still. It was already late. Finding and concealing the tape required to hold the charge against his chest, fitting the special plastic belt buckle behind which to hide the blasting caps, repacking his lunch pail to make room for the timer jar, scrounging around for the transistor radio—all these necessary preparations would take time. He would have to wait until Monday to disassemble the charge.

31

PAUL KNEW THAT CALLING HOME WAS HOPELESS, for they had had to pull all four telephones from their plug-in jacks just to have breakfast that morning. No sooner had he hung up on the crank than the phone had rung again: the local educational television station, asking for a taped interview. Then there had been an early-rising friend of Sherry's, wanting to commiserate, a man claiming the name of a nationally known conservative commentator, a CBS flunky who wanted to put him on "hold" while he roused the anchorman, and then a "breather." That was the clincher: the plugs came out.

"I can understand your reluctance to talk on the phone," the CBS factotum had sympathized, ignoring his protest that the Henderson column stated the whole issue, that there was nothing more he wished or intended to say. "We'll send out a camera crew."

So driving home was also out of the question. For all he knew, half a dozen such crews might well be waiting in ambush. And by evening their number would probably have doubled. Whether he spent the weekend granting the clamored-for interviews or refusing to grant them, the prospect was equally bleak. It was time to get away.

TIME FOR LOST WEEKEND STOP, he printed on the notepad before him, working out the message on the pay telephone's narrow gray shelf. MEET ME IN KROGER PARKING LOT 12:30 STOP LOVE PAUL STOP. He had decided to communicate with Sherry by telegram.

When he rang up Western Union with his message, he was informed that they had discontinued personal delivery years ago. "We telephone the message," the operator told him. "If we don't get an answer, we mail it."

"But that doesn't make any sense," Paul protested. "Why pay two or three dollars for a telegram when it's going to be handled just like a letter you can mail for a few cents?"

144

"It's the sense of urgency," the clerk replied. His ignorance had provided her with a chance to expound. "We didn't send more than a half dozen messages like yours last year. Most of our business comes from collection agencies . . ."

For a moment Paul held the telephone receiver at arm's length and stared at it in disbelief. The voice prattled on, tinny now that the earpiece was no longer against his head. He had unleashed a torrent.

"You'd be amazed . . ." the voice was saying when he returned the receiver to his ear, "at how many deadbeats who never paid ten bills in their whole life will suddenly cough up after getting a telegram. Puts the fear of God into them."

The woman's voice took on a pontifical tone and grew solemn. "It all goes back to the war, when telegrams brought death messages. People are so relieved to find out nobody's dead that they pay the bill as a sort of thanksgiving. All very complex," she added lamely, obviously getting beyond her depth. "Psychological." Paul could almost picture the woman, a matronly grandmother, nodding sagely to herself in the grimy, yellow-walled office.

"Yes," he interjected quickly, before she could get started again. "That's all very interesting. But I want a message delivered personally."

There was a pause. Then, unexpectedly, the woman offered a solution. "Say it with flowers." She chuckled. "They still deliver."

Turning into the parking lot, Paul saw Sherry's red Volkswagen parked near the store's entrance. She had seen him coming, and was standing on the car's running board, waving.

They embraced, laughing, as delighted with the success of their deception as two schoolchildren escaping from class with forged parental excuses.

"I was afraid there would be a bunch of reporters," he said.

"A bunch!" Sherry exclaimed. "Try fifty."

Paul found himself staring at her incredulously. "You're not serious."

145

"Serious." Sherry laughed. Then, her tone abruptly changing, she added, "Damned vultures."

"How did you manage to get away without being followed?"

Sherry's smile reappeared. "Elementary, my dear Watson." She laughed again. "I said I was going to the post office." She pointed, directing his eyes to a brown-paper-wrapped, string-tied package on the back seat. "Our luggage," Sherry explained. "You don't think I'd go off for a weekend with a man who didn't have a change of socks or shorts, do you?"

"I figured we'd smell so rank by the time we got back that they'd have to leave us alone." Paul grinned, impressed by her subterfuge. He leaned down and peered into the VW, where Katie sat quietly, still buckled into her seat. "Hi there," he smiled.

"Hi," Katie said.

"She's been a doll," Sherry said.

"You're always a doll, aren't you?" Paul said to Katie.

"Katie's always a doll," his daughter echoed archly. Paul was convinced she had an adult sense of irony. When he had shared that view with Sherry, she had called it further evidence of his hopeless dotage.

"I saw an advertisement in the *Bulletin of the Atomic Scientists,*" Paul told Sherry after they had transferred Katie and the package to the larger automobile. "A little college up in New Hampshire is looking for a nuclear physicist with exactly my background. I know some of the men in the department—they're good. But I've never seen the school." He switched on the car's ignition, put his hand on the gear shift, and then turned to meet Sherry's expectant eyes. "What do you say we drive up look it over?"

Sherry leaned across Katie and kissed him happily on the mouth. "Love it," she said.

146

32

WHEN LESTER ARRIVED at the Sand Beach Nuclear Plant at seven fifty-three Monday morning, the plastic buckle on his belt, tape on the skin of his back, and extra room in his lunch pail, it was a different world.

He sensed that something was wrong the moment he swung left off the highway onto the half-mile-long two-lane access road. There were parked cars everywhere, crowding the blacktop entrance road on either side, reducing two lanes to barely one. He drove through this corridor of multicolored steel with mounting unease. Where there were this many automobiles, there had to be a crowd of people, but where they were, or why, he could not imagine. Both questions were answered as he made the short right-hand turn that brought the Plant's main gate into view. The cars' human freight clogged the road ahead of him, brandishing placards, seething in amoebic ebb and flow.

Even as he spotted the clotted mass, it spied him, burped outward, grew tentacles, and encircled him.

"DON'T GO IN! DON'T GO IN!" The chanted command swept over him, growing louder, more insistent, more threatening. He brought the car to a halt, unable to advance through the enveloping press of humanity.

Then, just as suddenly, like a movie reversing itself, the crowd of protestors fell back. A phalanx of armed guards appeared, its leading wedge breaking through the crowd, its trailing edges dropping martinets who formed a temporary dike against the wash of bodies. The road was cleared; Lester accelerated. A moment later, he swept past two armed guards, through the double gate, and into the steel-fenced employees' parking lot.

Only as he was shakily locking the car doors did he connect the madness he had just witnessed with Paul Hanson's allegations about the Plant's safety. Pocketing the key to the automobile, he glanced again at the crowd beyond the wire-mesh fence. A regular madhouse, he concluded as he made his way toward Gate Security.

The man who checked him through was a stranger; Nolan Kline was nowhere in sight. "Let's see your driver's license," the unfamiliar security officer demanded. He was holding Lester's company-issued identification tag. For three years, that tag had been the sole identification required of any Sand Beach employee for entrance to the Plant.

"That's Lester, all right," a half-familiar voice piped up. Its owner was invisible behind the opaque one-way glass of the gatehouse.

The new guard ignored that assurance, persisting in his examination of Lester's driver's license. Then, without preamble, he punched a stopwatch on the desk before him, simultaneously demanding Lester's Social Security number.

"What?" Lester stuttered.

"State your Social Security number," the man repeated.

"Uh . . . five two five nine o five nine eight eight."

The man clicked the stopwatch, made a notation on the clipboard beside it, and motioned curtly. "Walk through the scanner."

Lester complied, the man made another notation, and he was motioned on. "Go ahead."

Lester had passed out of earshot when the voice inside the guardhouse mumbled, "That's funny. Lester's triggered the scanner every day for the past two months with that big cowboy belt buckle of his. Was he wearing it when you sent him through?"

"What the hell are you talking about?" the new security officer demanded.

33

EARL STAFFORD STARED SIGHTLESSLY at the telephone. Although the conversation had been concluded a full sixty seconds earlier, his face still wore a fading expression of incredulous disbelief.

On Friday, everything had seemed under control. Cal was right though, he should have gotten rid of Hanson the moment he wrote that letter to the NRC. It probably wouldn't have changed anything, but at least he wouldn't still be associated with the Company. People tended to mistrust the unemployed.

But that wasn't the half of it. Richards had just informed him that Rombart and Walter were turning chicken.

"No," Richards had commented sarcastically. "They don't admit to having changed their minds. It's just that neither is willing to categorically affirm that what Hanson says *might* happen *can't* happen." At that point, Richards had emitted a sharp, disagreeable laugh. "They called me ten minutes apart with the same story.

"It's not that they believe Hanson's allegations. Oh no. Not for a minute. They believe Sand Beach is perfectly safe. It's just that, *theoretically speaking*"—again there had been the sharp bark of laughter—*"theoretically speaking,* the sort of thing Hanson claims is possible, is, well, hypothetically speaking, just hypothetically, you understand . . . well . . . *possible."* The sneer in Richards's voice had been almost palpable.

"So they're not going to back us up?" Stafford had asked. That question, its answer self-evident from Richards's words, represented a sort of private, individual cultural lag. What had been, what ought to be, surely must actually be.

"Now you've got it," Richards had stated, flat-voiced. "They're the rats. And, buster, you better believe, you're the sinking ship."

Stafford hadn't wanted to ask the other question, but knew he had no choice. "What are you going to do?" he had asked, after several seconds of buzzing silence.

"I'm going to wait and see how the wind blows," Richards had replied. "If it starts blowing on me, I'm going to order the Plant shut down."

That reply was exactly why Stafford had put off asking the question. He had sent the problem to Accounting early Friday afternoon, as the worst of several unlikely and distasteful contingencies. The loss that would be incurred by the necessity of purchasing one hundred percent of Sand Beach's power from competing companies rounded off to half a million dollars a day.

"You can't do that," Stafford had protested. "The Plant's safe. There's no reason."

"You know that. I know that." Richards had agreed. "But it's irrelevant. Whorehouses are safe too. But if there's a stink, they get closed anyway."

"It could cost us a hundred million," Stafford had said. "We would have to skip our dividend."

What he had not said was far more significant. A skipped dividend meant a scapegoat, and the only scapegoat that would satisfy the stockholders in such a debacle was the corporation president. Being fired as President would cost him nearly a million dollars in lost stock options and bonuses, plus another million in severance and retirement benefits; not to mention the drop in market value of his common-stock holdings, which, as an insider, he was prohibited from dumping until news of the Sand Beach shutdown officially became public knowledge. If Richards shut down Sand Beach, Stafford stood to lose three million bucks.

"You can't," he had repeated, desperately, in a whisper.

Richards had responded cold-voiced and without sympathy. "Then you better start rounding up some experts. And you better make damned sure they won't go mush on you when it comes to the crunch."

34

A FEW MINUTES PAST TWELVE NOON, Lester casually ambled toward the first-floor elevator that would drop him to the sub-basement of the Diesel Generating Building, He expected to punch the button and have the elevator doors slide open. Instead, before he even got close enough to raise his hand to the switch, an unfamiliar security officer intercepted him, barring his way.

"What's goin' on?" Lester said.

"Who are you?" the security officer rejoined.

Lester tapped the identification tag clipped to his shirt pocket. "Lester Cuthright. Rad Protection Technician. I've gotta make some swipes."

"Sorry," the security officer stated, without sympathy or sorrow. "You're a pink tag. Only greens and blues are allowed into the lower levels. New policy."

"What?" Lester said. His mind could not even begin to digest the import of the security officer's statement—it was unthinkable.

"Greens and blues," the man repeated.

"But I gotta make those swipes," Lester protested. In his confusion and fear, he failed to hear the high, strained lilt in his voice.

The security officer was studying him intently. "Say," he said. "Ain't you the guy with the screwed-up kid?"

Only his knowledge of the bomb prevented Lester from attacking the man. Through the haze of rage the stranger's remark had evoked, Lester studied him, memorizing his features. He was most likely a local, and, if he was, he'd find him, sooner or later.

"I read your file," the man continued, grinning, giving Lester the fisheye. "How come you're so hot to get down below?"

"I ain't hot," Lester protested. He realized his eagerness

had made him suspect. "Just tryin to do my job." Jesus, he hated the bastard.

"Who are you, anyway?" he said to the guard. "Don't seem quite right, you knowin' my name, but me not knowin' yours."

"Gilbert," the man said.

Gilbert, Lester noted to himself; he wouldn't forget the name.

As he turned away, Lester tried to convince himself that it didn't matter. He'd just have to wait, hang loose, until all this excitement blew over. Then he would go in and take out the charge. There was no need to hurry, no reason to get uptight.

35

"THEY CHEERED ME," Paul told a bemused and faintly incredulous Sherry that Monday evening. "Like I was a goddamned hero."

"You've always been my hero," Sherry breathed with exaggerated adoration, snuggling closer to him on the couch.

Despite her irony, Paul could tell she was happy with him, and proud. He wished his own emotions were as uncomplicated and uncluttered with misgivings.

"It was wierd," he continued, more to himself than to Sherry, trying to come to grips with the experience. "You wouldn't have recognized the Plant. The access road was jammed solid with parked cars, all the way from the turnoff. Just one lane in the middle.

"There must have been two hundred people around the main gate, picketing, waving signs, yelling. They tried to stop me—they were doing that with every car that looked like it held Plant employees. And then someone must have recognized me, because I heard my name being shouted. And then, just like magic . . . I thought of Moses parting the Red Sea," he admitted, glancing away from Sherry's rapt gaze, embarrassed by that association, "there was suddenly an open lane, and I drove through to the gates of the parking lot. They stood on both sides and cheered.

"You should have seen the look I got from Claton when I walked into the Control Room," he added after a moment, relieved to return to a world of familiar motives and emotions. Still chagrined by his Red Sea metaphor, trying to atone, he laughed. "Speaking of biblical allusions, I think I'm the anti-Christ to Ron Claton. If looks could kill, I would've died on the spot."

They shared laughter, then grew silent. As that silence lengthened, the atmosphere in the room changed, the rosy glow of levity dissipating.

"What now?" Sherry asked, breaking the uncomfortably prolonged pause, her voice serious. Unconsciously, they pulled slightly away from each other. It wasn't withdrawal or antagonism, simply necessary distancing. She had asked a business question, and business and physical intimacy were basically incompatible.

Paul didn't answer immediately. Hunching forward on the couch, he rested forearms on knees and contemplated his clasped hands. When he finally responded, he spoke hesitantly, groping for a future impossible to predict with certainty, trying to sort out the probable from the merely possible.

"They missed their chance to fire me," he stated. "They should have done it right after the NRC meeting. They could have gotten away with it then, had me out of the way by now."

He glanced up and over his shoulder at Sherry, found the effort awkward, and straightened to rest his back against the couch, a position that allowed him to meet his wife's eyes more easily. "It would cause too much publicity now, and be too obvious a hatchet job. I expect they'll wait until this thing has blown over, one way or another. Then they'll work a lateral transfer on me. Get me out of the operations end and into a desk job in some out-of-the-way place. Then, after a respectable amount of time, they'll give me a generous severance bonus and slide me out.

"Actually, the timing should work out just about right. I figure they'll fire me sometime late in the spring or early on in the summer. So I'll go ahead and apply for that teaching position for next fall.

"That's item one. We'll have to sell the house, move, take a big cut in my salary—it'll be a hassle.

"Item two is what's going to happen at the Plant." His eyes met Sherry's somberly. "I think they're going to have to shut it down."

"What?" Sherry exclaimed in disbelief. "You told me yourself that at the NRC meeting—"

"That was before all this publicity," Paul interjected. "If you saw what was going on out there this morning, you'd understand. And the news coverage—it's been on every network news broadcast since Friday evening."

He leaned forward to the coffee table and picked up Monday morning's newspaper. "Did you see this?" he asked, indicating the boxed item on the lower left corner of page one.

Sherry nodded. "Yes."

"Eighty-four percent in favor of an immediate shutdown pending a full Congressional hearing," he said, summarizing the results of the telephone poll.

"Of course," he added, "the Company is trying to pour oil on the whole thing. You wouldn't believe the number of extra guards and security people they've hired; special security clearances to get into critical areas of the Plant; inspectors all over the place, inspecting like crazy—the whole bit. But I don't think it's going to wash, not with this much public pressure."

Sherry regarded him with dawning belief. Slowly, like the petals of a flower opening in the morning sun, her lips parted, and she smiled radiantly. "Then we've won!" she cried happily. "We've won!"

Despite himself, Paul found himself smiling in return. It wasn't exactly the sort of victory one stood up and crowed about. "That's the way it looks," he said.

36

AS LESTER DROVE AWAY from Sand Beach Monday evening, he acknowledged that there might be something to his mother's cherished superstition that everyone was born with a guardian angel. Something, at least, had been watching over him on this day. If they hadn't jacked up the security clearance for the Diesel Generator area, if he'd been able to get down there and take apart the charge as he'd planned . . . He could still scarcely believe how stupid he'd been. Maybe because it had all come up too quick, not giving him time to think it through.

Half an hour earlier, as he walked toward the parking lot, two security officers had intercepted him and escorted him back to the guardhouse. There Kline was waiting for him. As he was marched through the door, the bastard had eyed him with the oily smirk of a cat with one paw on a mouse.

Only after several minutes, when Kline tired of playing with him and came to the point, demanding that he remove his belt, had he realized his mistake: wearing the plastic buckle with no metal taped behind it, nothing to trip the scanner. Recalling Kline's demand, Lester experienced a brief flash of grudging admiration for the security guards. They didn't miss a trick; he had to give them credit for that. Wouldn't they have had a ball if he had been able to get down to the basement. With the plastic explosive on his back, blasting caps on his belt buckle, and timer in his lunch pail, he would have been a regular walking bomb. But, thanks to his luck, they had found nothing.

"You got two belt buckles just the same, Lester?" Kline asked as he fingered the imitation.

"That's right," Lester said. "Any law against that?"

"Didn't say there was, now did I?" Kline responded mildly. Lester didn't like the way Kline was running his fingers over the back side of the buckle, tracing its contours, caressing it. "But, you gotta admit, it's sorta unusual.

156

"Why do you have two buckles just the same, Lester?" Kline demanded, suddenly looking up, boring his eyes into Lester's. "I mean, just the same, 'cept one's plastic and one's metal?"

"I chipped the silver one," Lester answered, inventing the spur-of-the-moment tale as he talked. "Took it back to the shop to get it fixed. Got this one to tide me over. After all," he added, seeking a convincing conclusion, "you can't wear a belt without no buckle."

"What shop was that, Lester?"

Lester cursed to himself, then saw a way out. "Some western store downtown. Don't remember its name. But I ain't actually taken the silver buckle back there yet. Been meaning to."

Kline nodded agreeably, as if that cleared up his confusion, made everything perfectly clear.

"In that case, Lester," Kline commented after a few moments, "if you haven't been back to the shop, how come you've got this extra?"

Lester stumbled for only an instant. "Uh . . . just picked it up at some store—not the same store. You can get these plastic ones lots of places."

Kline studied the plastic buckle appraisingly. "I'm afraid I'm gonna have to ask you to get another buckle, Lester. Just a plain little buckle"—he pointed to his own waist—"like mine here." Then he smiled, a thin-lipped smile. "You see, Lester," Kline said. "It would just make too much work for my boys, having to take off your belt every day."

As he swung the car into the freeway exit lane, Lester consoled himself with the thought that it really didn't matter. He'd just have to forget about bringing out the caps, that's all. Suddenly he grinned. He would dump them into one of the waste containers scattered throughout the Plant. Part of Security's job was to screen the containers' contents before sending the garbage off to the dump. Finding those two caps would send them up the wall for a month.

157

37

GRUNTING, GROANING, AND MOANING, Dirk dragged himself out of bed at six o'clock Tuesday morning, a full hour earlier than usual. As he staggered across the bedroom to throttle the screaming alarm clock, he cursed Paul Hanson, the man responsible for his misery. If Monday was any sort of precedent, by eight the Plant's gate would be clogged with crazies. He had to get there first, leaving enough time before the onslaught to get things organized.

It was almost ten o'clock before he was finally able to enter his office and attack the accumulated backlog of paperwork. When he saw his desk, he cursed Hanson a second time. Normally, days would pass, sometimes entire weeks, without a single priority security report landing on his desk. This morning, there was a stack of such reports. Every empty threat shouted anonymously from the crowd outside the gate, every act of petty vandalism, every personal injury, however slight, had to be reported. Most likely, no true security threat was posed by any of these incidents. But it was his job to make sure of that, to screen the reports first thing before turning to other matters. As he drew his chair up to the desk, the pile centered neatly before him, he repeated the curse, appending an obscenity.

The first report on Cuthright was fourth down in the pile. It was more a memo than a report: a single page on which security officer Cy Gilbert succinctly described the apparent eagerness of one Lester Cuthright to enter the Diesel Generator area a few minutes past twelve noon on Monday. Gilbert recognized that the incident was probably without significance; nevertheless, he felt duty-bound to report it, in view of the subject's known antagonism toward the Company and the incongruousness of the subject's reaction upon being denied entry. For Cuthright had seemed upset when refused access, protesting a need to "make swipes" in the lower levels. While such con-scientiousness might be expected of a dedicated and ambitious employee, it struck Gilbert as curiously out of character, and thus possibly suspicious, coming from Cuthright.

Ringing Jill on the intercom, Dirk told her to pull Gilbert's file and find his date of employment. He had been transferred to Sand Beach on Saturday, Jill reported. Dirk was impressed. The man had apparently found time between Saturday and Monday to scan personnel files, and had remembered what he read. He made a mental note to remember the man the next time a position in the regular Security staff opened up. Since Cuthright had been kept out of the Diesel Generator area, and would continue to be denied entry to all critical areas of the Plant so long as the new regulations were in effect, Dirk felt no sense of urgency about solving the mystery of Cuthright's new-found dedication to his job.

It was almost eleven when Dirk reached the bottommost report in the stack: Nolan Kline's account of Cuthright's look-alike belt buckles. After reading the first two paragraphs, Dirk paused long enough to ring the guardhouse and order Kline to his office. He had just finished the remainder of the report when Kline knocked and entered.

"You're absolutely sure there was tape adhesive on the back?" Dirk's half-shouted demand was without preamble.

Frozen by the peremptory challenge, Kline stood just inside the room, his hand still on the door handle. His eyes flicked around, seeking the object of Dirk's question. But there were only the two of them. "What?"

"Shut the door, for Christ's sake!" Dirk commanded. Then, as Kline again faced him, he reiterated. "Cuthright. Yesterday. When you stopped him. Are you sure it was adhesive on the back side of his belt buckle?"

Comprehension and relief swept simultaneously across Kline's face. "Yes, sir. No doubt about it. I even managed to force some into a little roll. You know the way the stuff balls up when you rub it hard. It did that."

"What about the cock-and-bull story he fed you? Have you checked it out?"

Kline's unease began to rise again. "Well," he temporized, "not exactly—"

"What do you mean, 'not exactly'?" Dirk was faintly surprised at his own vehemence. But Kline was weaseling. "Have you or haven't you?"

"No, sir," Kline admitted. "I mean . . . I figured it showed he might've been up to something. But, after all, what can you carry behind a belt buckle?"

Dirk answered Kline's inane question with a hard stare. "If I knew, you'd be looking for it by now," he said.

"Me and the missus, we were invited to dinner at six yesterday," Kline belatedly confessed. "I was going to check it out today." He put on a tentative smile of chagrined apology, which didn't work.

Dirk felt no inclination to return Kline's smile, not with a mob of howling maniacs outside the gate, and Cuthright prowling around with God knows what from the back of that buckle.

Click. Gilbert's report. The Diesel Generator Building. It was beginning to add up. "But I know one thing. Whatever it is, he wants to get down to the diesels with it."

"Jesus," Kline muttered. Though he had no idea of the basis for Dirk's statement, he accepted its truth unquestioningly.

Dirk motioned his subordinate toward the door. "Use Jill's phone. Find that western store and check out Cuthright's story."

As Kline began to turn, Dirk added, "And tell Jill to bring me the bastard's file."

"Yes, sir," Kline said. But Dirk wasn't listening.

"The Cuthright file, sir." Jill said. Whether ten seconds or ten minutes had elapsed since Kline's exit, Dirk neither knew nor cared. He took the folder without looking up or breaking his trend of thought. Back to the strip search, he told himself. There were more clues now, more pieces in the puzzle, enough to form the outline of a picture. It was clear that Cuthright *did* have a reason to smile, that he *had* been up to something, even that long ago. But they had missed it.

He reread the "Strip-Search Inventory and Report" line by

160

line. As he studied it, he made notations on a yellow legal pad, trying to sift the wheat from the chaff. After ten minutes, he had a list:

Toggle-type belt buckle	——Switched to two large western-type buckles, one plastic, one metal. Why (Ans: To smuggle something into plant. Qu: What?)
Penknife in lunch pail	——Why in lunch pail instead of pants' pocket? (Ans: Slice food?)
Mortar dust in penknife mechanism	——Source?
Mortar dust, right hip pocket	——Source? How deposited in *hip* pocket?

Five minutes later still, when Kline strode back into the office, Dirk was still puzzling over the list. His only progress was the addition of a fifth entry:

Wants to transport some
thing small into
Diesel Generator Area——
What? Why?

"Sir." Kline said.

Reluctantly, Dirk's eyes left the list, rose to Kline's face, and found it flushed with eagerness. The man was obviously pregnant with information. He induced delivery with a nod.

"He bought both buckles the same day, at the same store," Kline exclaimed. "The plastic one *and* the metal one."

"You sure it was our Lester?" Dirk interjected.

Kline nodded vigorously, emphasizing his certitude. "No

doubt about it. When I described him, the clerk remembered him right off. Seems Lester didn't make a very good impression. Almost broke the counter top, acted rude." Kline grinned, then added irrelevantly, "I think the clerk's a fag. He and Lester didn't exactly hit it off, from what I gathered."

"Go on."

That curt command put a damper on Kline's self-contratulatory ebullience. When he continued, his tone was businesslike. "The clerk remembered two things that struck him as strange. Three, actually, because Lester wasn't, as he put it, their 'usual sort of client.' Anyway, he said that Lester was carrying a tape, and that the first thing he did when the clerk showed him the buckle was to measure it, both length and breadth."

"And?" Dirk demanded.

"That's what took me so long. I had to wait while the clerk hunted around for a tape measure." Dirk's impatient scowl penetrated his consciousness. "Three inches by four inches," Kline added hastily.

Dirk added the dimensions to his list. "Go on."

"The other thing the clerk thought strange was that Lester rejected the metal buckle at first—said it was too expensive—and asked if they had a plastic imitation. When the clerk brought it to him, Lester compared the two and then bought both buckles."

Dirk tried to decipher the puzzle. What was slightly smaller than three by four inches, and thin enough to fit behind a belt buckle without making a bulge? he asked himself. But no image formed. After a few moments, Kline's presence impinged on his awareness, and he issued an order. "I want Cuthright put under continuous surveillance. If he gets out of sight of a monitor, send a man to watch him. And if he does anything suspicious, take him into custody. You've got a perfect excuse, since he lied about those buckles. In fact," Dirk added, "we can fire him now. We've finally got cause."

"That's right!" Kline exclaimed. "I hadn't even realized that."

The knowledge that he had finally acquired the long-desired justification necessary to get rid of Cuthright forever brought Dirk surprisingly little pleasure. Once fired, Cuthright would be beyond his reach, would take his dirty little secret with him.

"But not today," Dirk said. "I want to find out what he's been up to." To do that he needed solitude, a chance to think. "Go get the surveillance started," he ordered.

As Kline turned to comply, Dirk returned eyes and attention to the scribbled list.

Mortar dust—hip pocket; mortar dust—penknife; penknife—lunch pail; buckle—something concealed.

There had to be a pattern, a picture, a meaning. But he couldn't get a handle on it.

Sensing a distracting tension, Dirk glanced down at his hands; they were clenching the arms of his chair with white-knuckled force. Relax, he told himself, it will all come together.

With deliberate effort, he made his hands go slack, then rocked back in his chair. Try for an innocent explanation first, he admonished himself, get away from the Plant.

He pictured Cuthright's house. White aluminum siding, wood trim. No brickwork; hence, no mortar. But he couldn't picture the foundation. That might be brick. Or the basement. Probably cinderblock there, with mortar between.

But he couldn't work up a credible picture of Cuthright picking away at the mortar in his own house with a penknife. It made no sense. He'd use a chisel, or, if he didn't have a chisel, a screwdriver.

But you don't know that, he reminded himself. Maybe the bastard doesn't even own a screwdriver. Picture him: in the basement, making a hole. He could see Cuthright now, a mental motion picture: picking away, then folding the knife, dropping it into his pants' pocket, and wiping his hands on his shirt front or slacks.

In his *pants' pocket!* The flash of insight was simultaneous with a surge of gut-wrenching animal terror like nothing Dirk had ever experienced.

Even as he fought to keep from retching, the sudden

intuition as staggering as a powerful physical blow, his mind clicked and chattered like a computer, spewing its conclusive printout, putting all the pieces into place.

If Cuthright was digging around at home, he would carry the knife in his pocket, at least part of the time; there would be traces of mortar dust in one of his trousers' side-pockets. But there weren't. He was using the knife to dig at something in the Plant; the handkerchief in his right hip pocket was his drop-cloth. That's where the mortar dust had come from. It hadn't shown up in the lab report because it had been washed out of the handkerchief. But the tight folds at the bottom of his hip pocket had held it.

"Holy mother of God," Dirk murmured. "Where?"

Like a movie unreeling hundreds of feet per second, Sand Beach projected itself in his mind, building by building, room by room, then froze in a single frame. The basement corridor in front of the Diesel Generator Room, over the power conduit, Cuthright sitting there, eating, lunch pail open at his side, and his right hand out of sight—with the knife.

Dirk never saw his secretary's startled spasm as he barged out of his office. He ran blindly through the reception area, making for Security Control. The two officers at the monitors jumped as Dirk crashed into the room, but he didn't register their actions either. "Where's Cuthright?" he demanded, already scanning the screens.

Before either man could respond, Dirk himself located Cuthright in the Reactor Service Building, making floor swipes.

"Arrest him," Dirk commanded over his shoulder, already on his way back to the flung-open door.

He saw nothing on his three-minute run through the Plant's labyrinthine corridors to the Diesel Generator Building—not the turned heads, not the amazed stares, not the half-fearful hops of people getting out of the way of his blind charge.

Only when he had clattered down the spiraling steel stairway and found himself actually standing in the very corridor his mind's eye had identified did Dirk momentarily pause. The

164

pounding of his heart, the rasp of his labored breathing impinged for the first time on his consciousness. As he strove to quiet them, he studied the brickwork shelf, trying to dredge from the three-month-old memory the exact spot where Cuthright used to sit.

Yes, he thought. That was it. About three feet out from the far wall. Aware that he was being observed by Security Control, Dirk forced himself to walk the length of the room. There was no point in playing the fool. For now that he was actually here, now that his judgment was about to be put to the test, he was assailed by sudden doubts. It was, after all, a hunch, an intuition, a gigantic inductive leap. If he was wrong, his panic of the last few minutes would provide behind-his-back humor for months to come.

When he stood opposite the segment of brickwork where Cuthright had sat, Dirk paused, hesitant to put his wild theory to the test. Then, prodded by the staring eye of the security camera, he stepped over the shelf. Wedging his legs into the narrow gap between brickwork and wall, he awkwardly knelt down and scanned the joints. A moment later, his face hidden from the television monitor by the top of the shelf, he smiled in triumph. There it was.

For an instant, before he touched the brick, Dirk felt a fleeting sorrow for Cuthright—he had him now. But victory made him mellow. The poor bastard would not only lose his job, he would go to prison. It was just as the warning signs posted everywhere around the plant declared: SABOTAGE IS A FEDERAL OFFENSE.

He studied the brick some more and noted that Cuthright hadn't even managed to get through all the mortar: the bottom joint was scarcely marred. The whole attempt was pathetic, another botched job, part and parcel with Cuthright's botched life.

Almost idly, not expecting it to move, Dirk gripped the brick and, out of simple unreflecting curiosity, gave it a tug. The blast of the exploding plastic hit him square between the eyes.

In the instant before he died, the last piece of the puzzle

fell into place, completing the picture. What was slightly smaller than three inches by four inches, metal, and thin enough to fit behind a belt buckle without making a bulge?

Blasting caps, Dirk thought.

DISASSEMBLY

38

IN THE SAND BEACH CONTROL ROOM, for almost three full seconds after the subterranean explosion in the Diesel Generator Building, normal routine prevailed. Had the pump-power and core-coolant-pressure monitors been properly wired, the Sand Beach reactor would have been completely scrammed by the end of that three-second period. Instead, the Period Meter and the core-coolant-temperature sensors were the first instruments to register the imminent disaster, and their readings were misinterpreted.

During seconds four and five subsequent to the severing of electrical power to the primary core-coolant pumps, the Junior Reactor Operator on duty treated the rise in reactor output as a typical power transient, to be routinely suppressed by minor control-rod adjustment. Not until six seconds after the explosion, simultaneous with a warning cry from the suddenly terrified junior operator, was automatic scram triggered. But by then the nuclear runaway was out of control.

The wail of the scram alarm was punctuated by two searing exclamation points as the indicator lights for both emergency-shutdown systems flared red. When the alarm sounded, Paul Hanson was standing before the primary instrument panel, idly discussing his inevitable transfer with Senior Reactor Operator Pete Owen, one of the few management-level personnel at the Plant who had remained friendly after the publication of Henderson's column. By the time he realized that the reactor had undergone an uncontrolled super-prompt-critical power transient, a matter of perhaps half a second, the partially inserted scram rods, aided by the Doppler effect, had terminated the overpower stage of the runaway. But, fifty feet below ground level, in the heart of the reactor core, the damage was irreparable.

Although outwardly intact and undamaged, showing no visible signs of the massive forces amok within its core, the two-billion-dollar Sand Beach liquid-metal-cooled fast-breeder reactor had commenced to destroy itself within milliseconds after the explosion of the diamond charge. Like a mortally wounded mako shark engorging its own spilled bowels, the reactor preyed on itself.

When, six seconds after the detonation of the C4 explosive, the reactor-period scram was automatically activated, the massive scram rods began their rapid descent—smooth, oiled, silent—but too slow. A few hundred milliseconds were required for full insertion; within one hundred milleseconds, they were jammed.

The fuel pins swelled, bulged, and then ruptured, spewing molten plutonium into the adjacent coolant channels. Cancer-like, the destruction spread through the core—pin dissolved pin, rod ate into rod, cluster devoured cluster. First in drops, then in rivulets, then in torrents, the flaming fuel fell, pouring into the stainless-steel bowl that constituted the reactor-vessel floor. There, in an alloyed caldron, the seething fuel hissed and bubbled.

The once magnificent core of the reactor, milliseconds earlier a delicate miracle of symmetry, resembled a vandalized stalactite cave. The plunging fuel-pin clusters, formerly arrow-straight spears of zirconium, were truncated, bowed, and broken. Thirty feet below that shattered roof lay the detritus: a molten moraine of mixed debris, intensely radioactive, roiling at a temperature of five thousand degrees Fahrenheit.

Ron Claton burst through the Control Room doors in apoplectic fury. "What have you done!" he screamed at Hanson. His words were not a question but an accusation.

"There's been a major power excursion," Hanson responded. "The core's disintegrating." He felt numb, almost in a state of shock. The gross core disassembly he had hypothesized was taking place at that very moment. They could be on the brink of a nuclear explosion. Yet Claton, in the grips of paranoiac idiocy, seemed oblivious.

"What do you mean, 'the core's disintegrating'?" Claton shouted. He was rushing across the breadth of the Control

Room like a lumbering lineman intent on a mid-field tackle. Just as Hanson tensed to leap aside, Claton brought himself up short and, instead of lunging, grabbed Hanson's shoulders in both hands and shook him. "What have you done, goddammit?" he demanded.

His own temper ignited by Claton's loutish stupidity, Hanson brutally broke the man's grip. "I haven't done a damned thing," he spat at the red, sweat-beaded face. "Can't you get that through your thick head?"

For a moment longer, Claton glared at him, unable to free himself from the fixated certainty that Hanson had deliberately wrecked the Plant.

"It just happened, sir," Pete Owen interjected. "Paul and I were talking, and all of a sudden it just happened." Like every other person in the room, the Senior Reactor Operator was standing. The scram alarm, like some sergeant's shouted command, had jerked each employee to stunned attention.

Then, almost simultaneously, various personnel recollected their proper duties. The *tableau vivant* of rigidly frozen postures dissolved. The insistent, piercing wail of the scram alarm, momentarily forgotten, reentered their collective consciousness.

"Turn that damned thing off," Claton commanded, and the alarm was silenced. Only then, in the ringing silence that ensued, did they hear the intercom's comparatively muted warble, a special melody signifying a priority communication.

Pete Owen stepped up to the intercom speaker and punched the flashing button. "Yes?"

"This is Security," a voice said. "Is Mr. Claton there?"

Shouldering Owen aside, Claton stepped toward the speaker. "Claton here."

"Girrard, sir," the voice announced, identifying itself. "We have Cuthright in custody. Dirk's dead . . . we think."

Hunching forward, Claton gripped the polished aluminum sill of the control-panel shelf with splayed hands. Then, like a tired and disoriented, yet determinedly undaunted bull, he lowered his head toward the speaker. With deliberate slowness, he demanded, "What are you talking about, Girrard?"

171

"The explosion in the Diesel Generator Building, sir," Girrard responded. "We think it killed him. We were watching on the monitor when it went off. Looked like it got him right in the face." The voice stumbled for a moment, stopped. Then Girrard added weakly, "There's stuff all over the wall. We're not sure, since the film's black and white . . ." He stumbled again. "But we think it's his head."

Despite the fragmentary, almost kaleidoscopic quality of Girrard's account, the sequence of events was perfectly clear to everyone in the Control Room near enough to overhear his words.

Hanson realized that Dirk had suspected Cuthright of sabotage. But he obviously had not presumed that Cuthright might have already succeeded in planting a bomb. Had he entertained that notion, he would never have been so careless as to detonate it. Yet detonate it he obviously had: hence the loss of power to the coolant pumps, hence the meltdown. And hence, Hanson added to himself, faintly chagrined that it came almost as an afterthought, Dirk's death.

"Has Cuthright made any admission?"

"No, sir," Girrard responded. "But he wants to call his lawyer. Should we let him?"

"It's his right," Claton observed. "Can you tape the call without him knowing it?"

"Yes, sir."

"All right. You do that." Wearily, drained of energy, Claton punched the "disengage" button and then levered himself up. The full weight of the disaster was beginning to make itself felt.

First, he would have to make phone calls, at least a dozen—to the Home Office, to the NRC, to the FBI, to the local police, to the press . . . There would be interviews, inquests, hearings, committees, investigators, examiners, inspectors . . . The future loomed in his mind's eye as one protracted inquisition, an interminable third degree with him, Ron Claton, forever beneath the burning lights.

He squelched the depressing vision, glanced around, and found himself standing alone. Everyone in the room seemed engaged in some purposeful activity. That impression reminded him that even though the reactor had lost its ability to produce electricity, it remained a potent force.

Too weary to work up his usual hate at Hanson's disloyalty, Claton drew a chair up next to him and asked what was happening. He knew his telephone calls would entail a status report.

"I think we're going to witness the China Syndrome," Hanson commented, speaking in his normal voice. The numbness he had felt immediately following the scram alarm was now almost completely dissipated. The computer-activated digital clock recessed into the control panel read "SCRAM + 2.36" minutes—he had monitored it even while listening to Girrard's report. When it had gone past 2.00 minutes, and the Reactor Containment Building still had its roof, he realized he had been wrong. The upper half of the reactor core was now substantially below criticality. The core crashdown he had feared, with its potential for explosive autocatalysis, had not occurred.

"China Syndrome?" Claton said. The term struck a faint chord somewhere in the back of his mind, but he couldn't quite dredge it out.

"There hasn't been much written about it lately," Hanson observed. "Had its heyday back in the late sixties and early seventies." He made a notation on the pad before him, recorded the time, and then glanced briefly at Claton. "It's the theory that, in a major meltdown, the molten fuel will eat its way through the bottom of the reactor vessel and the hot liner, through the reactor foundation, and on down into the ground right through to China.

"Silly name," he observed, more to himself than to Claton. "Once the fuel got to the center of the earth, it would have to melt its way up against the force of gravity. But, in theory, the fuel could go all the way to the earth's core and then just bubble down there until it finally wore itself out."

Claton regarded his Operations Supervisor incredulously. "You're not serious," he said. "You're not really suggesting that's what's going to happen."

Hanson smiled without looking up from the control panel. "No. But I wouldn't be surprised if the fuel went down fifty or sixty feet."

He tapped the plexiglass cover of one of the temperature monitors in the bank before him: it read "3200°." "That sensor is located about five feet up from the botton of the reactor vessel, so you can imagine what the heat must be like farther down. What we've got is a big stainless-steel soup bowl holding at least thirty tons of molten sodium and plutonium at temperatures up to five thousand degrees. With that heat, the soup bowl's surely melting. I'd say ten minutes, maybe fifteen, before the stuff eats through the base of the reactor vessel, then another twenty minutes or so to breach the hot liner. From then on, it will go down like a hot poker through a block of butter."

His lecture completed, Hanson sat back and smiled at Claton with genuine pleasure. This was a momentous event; it was no time for petty antagonisms. He felt no regret at the destruction of his career. He had been wrong about the explosion hazard; it was both right and inevitable that he should pay for that error. In the interim, however, he was privileged. "We're making history," he commented. "Things are happening in the reactor core that have never before happened anywhere in the world."

39

As Ron Claton made phone calls in his office and Paul Hanson monitored the decay heat in the intact upper half of the fuel assembly in the Control Room and, heavily guarded, Lester Cuthright protested his innocence and, outside the Plant's main gate, a few of the more alert placard-bearing protestors noticed a new grimness in the security officers' behavior, the pool of water trapped beneath the reactor's hot liner was absorbing immense quantities of heat.

The pipe fitting whose threads Clyde Jones had stripped years before had begun to leak some four months after the Sand Beach installation passed its final safety survey and became operational. At that time, the water pipe had been subjected to a routine pressurization test and had revealed no flaw. However, even if the leak had already existed when the pipe was tested, it is unlikely that it would have been detected. The rate of water loss was no more than a quart per hour, so the inspector would have to have been unusually patient, or his instrument especially delicate, in order to have discovered it. Since the pipe was classified as a non-critical assembly, both patience and delicacy of instrumentation were employed elsewhere: the pipe was tested for gross failure only.

Even toward the end, the leak was not large. It produced a fine, needlelike spray similar to that around the spigot of an insufficiently tightened garden hose. But over the three-year period that elapsed between the beginning of the leak and the destruction of Sand Beach, the effects of that fine, sharp spray were quite dramatic, a classic example of the erosive potential of a steady stream of water, however slight that stream might be.

It helped, of course, that the concrete in which the pipe was embedded was of inferior quality. That porous, coarse, and uncohesive concrete eroded readily. By the time the melt-down occurred, the little water jet had leached away some three score cubic feet of concrete. It had hollowed out a little cave whose roof was the reactor's hot liner, and had filled that little cave with water.

When the molten mixture of plutonium and sodium breached the reactor vessel and spilled into the hot liner, the liner's stainless-steel floor absorbed heat. Because of the thickness of the shield, several minutes passed before the underside of the liner registered a notable change in temperature and began to transfer thermal energy to the cold little lake.

Ironically, even if the existence of the water-filled cavity had somehow been revealed to those in the Control Room at this point, they would have been unable to prevent or alter the subsequent sequence of events. Only dispersal of the seething, liquefied fuel could have prevented what ensued.

Fifteen minutes after the scram alarm first sounded, the monitoring instruments in the Control Room continued to record the reactor's condition as essentially stable. The slight recorded change that had occurred seemed to point toward an amelioration of any potential danger. The major wave of decay heat in the still-intact upper fuel rods, though at first rising dangerously high, had been absorbed without initiating additional cladding failure.

However, beyond the reach of human eyes and instruments, unsuspected and undetected, at the bottommost convexity of the hot liner, the situation was not stable. The underside of the liner gleamed ruby red, irradiating the subterranean pool with crimson light and casting fiery shadows across the mouth of the miniature grottos and tunnels which pockmarked the cavern's concrete floor and walls. The temperature of the water filling the cavity had stood at forty degrees when the meltdown occurred. It now stood at three hundred degrees, and was rising at the rate of almost a full degree every second. Simultaneously, succumbing to the heat of the molten plutonium fuel, the hot liner was melting. It was melting slowly, giving up its surface millimeter by millimeter. But it was melting nonetheless, and growing progressively weaker.

176

40

IT IS DIFFICULT to conceive of water as a powerful explosive in itself, much less as the trigger for an explosion. Perhaps its mundane familiarity breeds contempt; perhaps the human mind rebels at the notion of the key life-giving substance as a life-destroyer; perhaps, associated as water is with the quenching of conflagrations, it violates common sense to see in it a source of devastation. Whatever the explanation, its potential power is seldom appreciated.

But not everyone makes that misjudgment. Any wartime sailor who has witnessed exploding boilers blast the guts out of a battleship, much less any sailor aboard such a ship when armored steel decks buckle and burst like bubble gum, knows the true power of steam, and fears it.

No ship's boiler, however mighty, ever began to approach in thickness or in strength the hot liner shield at Sand Beach. Nor had the water in any boiler ever been subjected to such heat as was now being injected into the pool beneath that shield. Nor did the crude boiler beneath the Sand Beach reactor possess a safety valve. It would continue to absorb heat until the pressure against the bottom of the stainless-steel shield reached thousands of pounds per square inch. Finally, inevitably, the boiler would explode.

That explosion would have the force of several hundred pounds of TNT. But in the Sand Beach reactor, such a steam explosion would be but the trigger for a far more powerful blast. For liquid sodium reacts violently with water, releasing immense quantities of hydrogen gas. So vast and so unthinkable was the explosive potential of tons of superheated sodium suddenly injected with a large quantity of water vapor that such a calculation had not even appeared in the mandatory safety evaluation for the Sand Beach installation. And with good reason: there was no economically feasible way an explosion of such magnitude could be contained.

The reactor vessel would become a gigantic mortar, the projectile its head. Hurled upward by the force of the explosion, the reactor head—some twenty tons of plate steel, control-rod drives, and refueling machinery—would impact the roof of the containment dome, breach it, and thereby inject into the atmosphere radioactive debris equivalent to the radiation released by the detonation of some three hundred Nagasaki-yield atomic bombs. Those Sand Beach employees at work inside the various Plant service buildings would have sufficient time to retreat to each building's euphemistically titled "Life Support Systems Area," there to await rescue in relative comfort and total security. But those employees unfortunate enough to be caught on the grounds when the containment was breached—the security personnel at the gate, and, of course, the protestors they were attempting to control—would all receive lethal doses of radiation within seconds of the explosion.

This explosion occurred without warning at 11:48 that Tuesday morning, precisely 32.073 minutes after the scram alarm first sounded.

EPILOGUE

FOR HIS FORESIGHT in ordering aloft the radiation-monitoring drone, Colonel Arthur Dudley subsequently received a special Presidential commendation and was jumped from near the bottom to the very top of the promotion list. The Colonel's decisive action was considered especially indicative of his leadership potential for having been made, in the absence of the Base Commander, on his own initiative. Colonel Dudley never revealed to anyone that he had assumed "nuclear excursion" was synonymous with "nuclear penetration" and so, in ordering the drone aloft, had simply been following the standard operating procedures which were rigidly prescribed for the latter, though not the former, eventuality.

In any event, the fortuitousness of Colonel Dudley's error extended far beyond its benefit to his career. It was theorized that, had he followed standard operating procedure and delayed scrambling the drone until word of the breakout itself was received, the number of casualties would have been increased by a factor of at least two, and possibly by a factor of three.

As it was, the plane arrived over the Sand Beach nuclear plant only six minutes after the reactor exploded. By flying a rapid search pattern downwind to the southeast, aided by its automated radiation monitors, the drone located the invisible nuclear cloud released by that explosion within thirty seconds. From that point on, the disaster went entirely according to plan.

The drone searched out the fanlike front of the radioactive cloud and thereafter flew back and forth, crisscrossing its steadily expanding breadth. As it did so, ground coordinates, keyed to radiation-level readings, were automatically transmitted to Base Command, where they were plotted by computer and projected on a situation board. On the basis of this information, emergency Civil Defense broadcasts instructed citizens to make their way to fallout shelters, identified the location of fallout shelters in the vicinity, and estimated the time available before the radioactive cloud would reach them. Helicopter-deployed troops, Martianlike in bulky radiation suits and filter-equipped face masks, quickly established the roadblocks necessary to quarantine the affected area, preventing contaminated vehicles and personnel from transporting their deadly patina of radioactivity into outlying regions. It was necessarily brutal, and some panicky civilians had to be shot. But, most importantly, it was effective.

In addition to its radiation-monitoring devices and complementary on-board computers, the plane was also equipped with a lead-shielded, swivel-hinged, black-and-white television camera, housed within a plexiglass bubble on its underbelly. It was recognized that at night the camera would be useless; but, it had been argued, there was a 63 percent likelihood that any given mission would be conducted during daylight. Assuming a mission was mounted during daylight hours, the instant visualization of ground-level activities which the camera would provide might well prove useful, and the installation would increase the plane's cost by no more than two hundred fifty thousand dollars. That defense of the system—potential usefulness reinforced by economy—overrode all minor objections. The camera, with appropriate reception and projection apparatus at Base Command, had been included in the aircraft's specifications.

The "big picture" however, was communicated on the situation board. That was where the overall pattern of the drifting, dispersing radioactive cloud showed up: its advance rate, breadth, and reactivity. The only things revealed by the television monitor were details: particular roads, cars, fields, houses—and people. Thus, it was scarcely surprising that no one was watching the monitor when, for a space of three seconds, the plane's television camera picked up Sherry and Katie Hanson, two diminutive figures standing beside a half-completed snowman, staring skyward at the funny-looking, low-flying aircraft. According to the figures on the situation

182

board, ground-level radiation at this location was a deadly three hundred roentgens per hour.

* * *

As Lester methodically refilled the hypodermic syringe, he recalled the words with which the physician, years ago, had handed him the authorizing prescription. "No one would blame you if you made a mistake," the doctor had said. "It would be human nature. You're not trained, after all. Eric could twist, and you could hit the heart before you'd even realized what you had done."

Grimly, he had shaken his head.

"I'd be willing to testify to that effect, if it came to that," the doctor had added.

"No," he had said. "Thanks anyway." Yet now that was how it was going to be, after all.

He had been grudgingly released after five weeks of incarceration, a period finally ended by the total failure of police efforts to unearth hard, incontrovertible evidence against him. Yes, of course, he had sat on the brick shelf in the vicinity where the explosion had occurred, but so had other personnel in the days and weeks before the blast. No, he had not planted the explosive. Yes, he was perfectly willing to submit to a polygraph examination. And he passed it.

Had a psychiatrist been employed to conduct a series of so-called affective-functioning tests on Lester, the reason for this seemingly impossible result would have become clear. For Lester was emotionally anesthesized, totally incapable of affective response—it was the only way his psyche could survive.

He had contemplated suicide while still in custody. But, before he could act, word had come that both Rachel and Eric had been institutionalized, and he had resolved to wait. Though he could do nothing to lessen the suffering of the hundred thousand burned and seared by the Sand Beach radiation, the two hundred thousand more who would succumb to radiation-induced cancer within a few years, the untold thousands of children who would be born deformed as a direct result of the explosion, he could at least end the suffering of his wife and son.

Rachel stirred slightly in her stupor as Lester injected the first syringe into her abdomen. By the time he had finished injecting the sixth, she had ceased to breathe. Eric, whether because his body had grown accustomed to hypodermic needles or because he was already too heavily drugged to register faint pain, did not stir at all.

Lester covered each body with a blanket, then turned toward the garage. He had decided against using the needle on himself, for fear of losing consciousness before he could inject a lethal dosage. The hose from the exhaust pipe to the rag-sealed window was already in place.

Facing the tiers of attentive faces before him, but not seeing them, Paul Hanson stood behind the lectern, addressing the class by rote in a dry, flat, inflectionless voice. He was no longer the youthful, robust man he had been two years before, when Sand Beach exploded. Having lost more than sixty pounds, he was now unnaturally thin, painfully so, wasted-looking. Since he had abandoned sports and recreation, his face, all bone and sharp angles, had grown sallow, displaying a yellowish cast like that of a person afflicted with jaundice. His hands, which clasped either side of the lectern, trembled slightly, as with palsy.

Hanson had never thought to question the popularity of his classes, the seemingly rapt attention with which his dry, atonal lectures were received; he accepted the fact without curiosity or interest, as he had accepted everything since Katie's and Sherry's death.

His colleagues at the university were more prone to speculation. Of several conflicting theories, the one most widely held maintained that students flocked into Hanson's classes not to be edified about physics, but out of morbid fascination at the spectacle of a man quite literally dying of grief.

184